SHANA NORRIS

SOMETHING TO
BLOG
ABOUT

SOMETHING TO BLOG ABOUT

AMULET BOOKS
NEW YORK

012391246Z

Library of Congress Cataloging-in-Publication Data:

Norris, Shana.
Something to blog about / by Shana Norris.
p. cm.
Summary: When pages from tenth-grader Libby Fawcett's password-protected blog are posted all over Yeardley High by her nemesis Angel Rivera, whose father is dating Libby's mother, the whole school finds out her humiliating secrets, as well as those of her friends and acquaintances.
ISBN 978-0-8109-9474-4 (hardcover with jacket)
[1. Interpersonal relations–Fiction. 2. High schools–Fiction. 3.Schools–Fiction. 4. Blogs–Fiction.] I. Title.

PZ7.N7984So 2008
[Fic]–dc22
2007013292

Text copyright © 2008 Shana Norris
Book design by Chad W. Beckerman

Printed and bound in U.S.A.
10 9 8 7 6 5 4 3 2 1

HNA
harry n. abrams, inc.
a subsidiary of La Martinière Groupe
115 West 18th Street
New York, NY 10011
www.hnabooks.com

For Mom and Dad.
And for my husband.

Acknowledgments:

First I'd like to thank my agent, Stephen Barbara, and my editor, Tamar Brazis, for loving Libby as much as I do and giving so much of their support. Thank you also to everyone at Abrams for your talent and hard work, and for giving me such a great home.

A special thank you to Libby's first readers and cheerleaders: Jenny, Angela, Rachel, Libbet, Laurie, Kristal, Caysie, Sabrina, Hanna, Crystal P., and Crystal H. Thanks also to Marlene Perez, Emily Marshall, Tamra Westberry, and Teri Brown for all of your valuable advice. A big thank you to everyone at Forward Motion, the blue board, and the teenlitauthors group.

Never-ending thanks to my family and friends, for always encouraging me to follow a dream. And thank you especially to my husband, for putting up with the cast of characters that lives inside my head.

SOMETHING TO
BLOG
ABOUT

SOMETHING TO BLOG ABOUT

● ABOUT
● RECENT POSTS
● SEPTEMBER
● OCTOBER
● NOVEMBER
SO GOOD-BYE
ISN'T FOREVER
BIG HEADS
AND GRANNY
PANTIES

My journey into online journaling began with one little entry written on the day that my normal, boring life *literally* went up in flames.

You see, I didn't carry a notebook that I could lose or leave wide open for anyone to find. I learned my lesson when I was in second grade. One day in class, I wrote on the back of my worksheet "Sara Masters is mean and has a big head" in huge purple-crayon letters. I was mad that she hadn't invited me to her birthday party even though I had invited her to mine the summer before.

As you might guess, I lost the worksheet. Jenny Sutton found it and showed it to Sara, who cried and told our teacher. (It wasn't like I was lying or anything. Sara really *did* have an abnormally large head for a seven-year-old.)

1

SOMETHING TO BLOG ABOUT

But my blog was different. It was password-protected specifically so another incident like that wouldn't happen.

Looking back, I guess putting it online wasn't the best idea, but having a blog made it so easy to add entries whenever I wanted, even while I was at school. And I could type faster than I could write in a diary anyway. I started the blog just to get out all the thoughts that were jumping around in my head about the various disasters in my life. I never imagined that it would become the cause of a much bigger drama.

I should have known something would happen eventually. Angel has always tried to ruin my life. For example, today she announced in a loud voice that my dingy granny panties were hanging out of the waistband of my pants. In the cafeteria. In front of my friends and nearly half of the kids at school.

- ABOUT
- RECENT POSTS
  - SEPTEMBER
  - OCTOBER
  - NOVEMBER

SO GOOD-BYE ISN'T FOREVER

BIG HEADS AND GRANNY PANTIES

2

Figures she'd decide to do that on laundry day, when all my nice underwear was in the washing machine.

Sometimes, even passwords can't keep out the person whose only goal in life is to make you miserable . . .

3

SOMETHING TO BLOG ABOUT

THURSDAY, SEPTEMBER 27, 2:01 PM
GIRL ON FIRE

Going back to school is completely out of the question. I can never show my face—along with what's left of my hair—in the halls of Yeardley High EVER again. I know this probably isn't the right way to start out an online journal. According to the oh-so-helpful and not-at-all-lame instructions on this blog site, I'm supposed to introduce myself (Libby Fawcett—don't call me Elizabeth) by writing my age (fifteen) and all this other stuff about me.

But since this blog means I can write private entries that no one besides me can ever read, why should I bother with formalities? Besides, it's pretty hard to focus on stuff like that now that my life is COMPLETELY OVER.

The morning started out innocently enough. I had morning breath that tasted like I'd been eating socks in my sleep and I found a pimple on my earlobe. I covered it up with a dab of

SOMETHING TO BLOG ABOUT

foundation that was so old it had separated inside the bottle. That made my earlobe look dirty, like I couldn't be bothered to wash it while I was in the shower washing everything else, so I brushed some three-year-old blush over it, hoping that it would brighten up the foundation.

My best friend, Keisha, swore she couldn't see anything when I pointed my ear out to her. Roger (my cousin) says I obsess over the tiniest details of my appearance and notice things that no one else would ever see if I didn't make such a big deal out of them.

But really, who gets a pimple on their EAR?

Certainly not Angel. She walked into the girls' room after first period to find me leaning over one of the sinks, staring at the eruption on my ear in the dirty mirror.

"Ew," she said as she continued over to one of the stalls. "If you're popping

● ABOUT
● RECENT POSTS
● SEPTEMBER
GIRL ON FIRE

5

something, Elizabeth, wipe your gunk off the mirror before you leave the room."

I hate when she calls me Elizabeth and she knows it. Angelina Rivera takes every available opportunity to torment me. In kindergarten, our teacher gave each student a pack of blocks at the beginning of the year to use for math exercises and Angel threw mine in the trash when no one was looking. I was accused of being a thief and taking the blocks home. Angel sat at her desk the whole time, not saying a word, while I cried in front of the entire class.

She has been my sworn enemy since that moment.

And I'm sure she will never, NEVER let me live down what happened today.

● ABOUT
● RECENT POSTS
● SEPTEMBER
GIRL ON FIRE

I HAD FOURTH-PERIOD CHEMISTRY CLASS with my best friend, Keisha Jones, and my cousin, Roger Fawcett. *And* with Seth Jacobs, the object of my eternal lust.

We were doing lab work that day in class, which I despised. Chemistry was my worst subject. It was just over a month into the school year and I was already in danger of failing.

"What do we add in now?" Keisha asked as she lit the flame for the Bunsen burner.

I tore my gaze away from Seth, who sat in the back of the room with his partner, Janet Li. He was playing with the flame from his burner, swinging his fingers back and forth through it.

"Oh, um . . ." I looked down at my instructions sheet for a moment and then turned to Keisha. "What step are we on?"

"What step am *I* on, you mean," Keisha muttered, grabbing the sheet from me. "I'm doing all the work while you drool over the table."

What had crawled up Keisha's butt and died? It wasn't like I hadn't ever put up with her crushes.

"I'm not drooling." I wiped my chin to make sure and then snatched the sheet back. "I'll finish the work myself."

Keisha laughed. "Sorry, Libby, but I really don't feel like being blown up today because you're more interested in the chemistry between you and Seth than in chemistry *class.*"

"What is your problem?" I asked.

"Nothing's my problem," Keisha said. "I just need a good grade on this project and it would be *nice* to have a partner who helps."

I turned around in my seat to face the front of the room. "No problem. All you had to do was say so. What do we do next?"

I tried to focus on the work, I really did. I needed an A in chemistry to bring up my average. But I found myself looking over my shoulder toward the back of the room again. Seth held a pair of tongs over the flame and watched the metal blacken. Janet kept scowling at him, clearly unappreciative of the interesting ways that Seth chose to express his boredom.

Seth grinned at Angel Rivera. She sat at the table next to him with Roger, who was her partner. She said something I couldn't hear, causing Seth to laugh. Angel laughed, too, and subtly shifted her chair closer to him. All the other guys in class watched Angel, probably wishing she showed them as much attention as she showed Seth. Unfortunately, she was gorgeous, with long, silky black hair and golden brown skin. The boys of Yeardley High were crazy about her and followed her around, doing whatever she told them to. But Angel always paid more attention to Seth.

Almost every girl in school liked him, but Seth never dated anyone. He did plenty of flirting and smiling—at least he did with the pretty girls. Needless to say, he never gave me a second look.

Just as that thought crossed my mind, Seth did look at me. And smile. He was smiling at Angel, and then he turned his head, still smiling as he looked around the room. His gaze met mine for a moment, until I had to look away—my face suddenly felt as if it were on fire.

I had loved Seth ever since we worked on a group project together in eighth-grade English. We had to draw a scene from *Animal Farm* and Seth had told me that my pig looked very "lifelike." A lame compliment, I know, but after that moment my heart belonged to him.

I barely listened to Keisha as she read the chemistry instructions out loud. Instead, I imagined what it would be like to kiss Seth, to run my hands through his sandy blond hair and have his arms around me. To have him—

"Libby!" Keisha's shriek shattered my daydream.

Before I could open my mouth to ask what I had done wrong this time, Keisha pushed at my shoulders, sending me and the wooden stool I'd been perched on down to the floor. She danced around like some crazed banshee, shrieking and hitting me with her notebook.

Then Ms. Hoover leaped at me and practically smothered me with a blanket. It felt as if a hundred hands were slapping me through the fabric. I struggled on the floor, trying to push the blanket and swat the hands away.

"Hey!" I cried. "That was my nose!"

Ms. Hoover pulled the blanket off and let me sit up. "Are you all right?" she asked.

A stench filled the air. It reminded me of the time I had gotten my hair caught in my mom's hair dryer.

My hands flew to my head. The charred clump of hair I found crumbled into wisps at my touch. I stared at the blackened bits in my hand, my mouth hanging open as my brain tried to sort out what had happened.

"You leaned over the burner," Keisha told me.

Roger stood behind her, his face white. "Are you okay?"

The entire class stared at me as I cupped my burned hair with my hand. I couldn't bear to look, so I kept my gaze locked on the toes of my old pink sneakers.

"Can I go to the office?" I asked.

"Are you sure you aren't hurt anywhere else?" Ms. Hoover asked in a soft tone I'd never heard her use before. Great, I'd made such a complete idiot of myself that even cranky old teachers felt sorry for me.

"I'm fine," I said, feeling the first sting of tears forming in my eyes. I had to get out of that classroom *immediately*.

"Do you want me to go with you?" Keisha asked as she watched me gather my books and backpack.

I shook my head as Ms. Hoover handed me a note excusing me from class. I hurried out of the room, but I still heard the snickers behind me before the door swung closed.

When I got to the office, I dialed my mom's work number.

"McMillen Family Medicine," said a voice that wasn't my mom's. My mom usually answered the phone.

"Hi," I said, trying to keep my voice steady. "May I speak with Maura Fawcett, please?"

"I'm sorry. Maura has stepped out for a moment. Would you like to leave a message?"

I glanced at the clock on the wall to see what time it was. Eleven sixteen. What was Mom doing away from work so early?

Since my mom refused to get a cell phone—thinking the cell companies had all conspired together to charge outrageous rates that they knew the gadget-greedy public would pay—I couldn't call her directly, wherever she was.

"Yes, thank you," I said. "This is her daughter, Libby. Tell her to come pick me up immediately. There's been an 'incident' at school."

I didn't realize how cryptic that message sounded until Mom burst into the main office almost twenty minutes later. She panted heavily, as if she had run all the way across town, and her brown curls stood up all around her head in a frizzy crown. She still wore her scrubs and white tennis shoes; her purse was clutched in one hand.

"Where's my daughter?" she gasped. When she caught sight of me sitting on a chair along the wall, she rushed forward and fell to her knees at my feet.

"Are you okay? What happened? Are you hurt?" Her

hands pawed over my shoulders, arms, and legs, checking for any sign of injury. The school nurse had already checked me over while I was waiting and she determined the only thing that had burned was my hair. She said I was *lucky.* Ha.

I pointed at my head without a word. Mom's gaze roamed over my hair, her eyes widening at what she saw. One half of my brown hair was still shoulder length and smooth. The other half was burned—the longest strands just barely reaching my chin and the ends shriveled into blackened curls.

Mom reached out to touch the charred remains of my hair, but stopped, her hand hovering only inches from the damage. "What happened?"

I could usually talk to my mom about anything. It had been just the two of us since before I was even born, ever since my dad left when he found out my mom was pregnant. I had told my mom about my first kiss and even about Keisha's first kiss. (Keisha would kill me if she ever found out that I had told my mother.)

But right then, I wasn't in the mood to talk about anything, especially the reason I wasn't paying attention in class. So I just said, "I had an accident involving a Bunsen burner."

Mom knew when I didn't want to talk, so she didn't ask

for details. She simply nodded and signed me out of school for the rest of the day.

I stretched out across the gray cloth backseat of our car, using my backpack as a pillow, while Mom got into the front and started the ignition. I watched the tops of trees and buildings pass by outside the window as we drove through town. Mom played with the radio for a moment. A big truck rumbled by as we waited to make a left turn. Everything else in the world was normal. Every*one* else was normal. I was the only freakshow who burned her hair.

"Do you want to go to Andrea's to see if someone can fix it?" Mom asked.

"No one can fix me," I told her. "I'm defective. Trade me in for a graceful daughter."

"A graceful daughter wouldn't be my Libby." ,

I remained silent.

"That was a joke, Libs."

Couldn't my own mother see that I wasn't in the mood for jokes? Plus, I never handled teasing very well.

At Andrea's Salon, an old, blue-haired woman looked at us over the top of the magazine she was reading. I kept my eyes on my feet, but I could feel her staring at my hair. I wished I could hide.

Mom went to speak to the receptionist, so I slumped into an empty chair.

"I put both our names on the list," Mom told me as she sat down. "I could use a trim."

I grabbed a huge book of hairstyles and held it open in front of my head.

"It's not that bad," Mom said.

"Excuse me for not believing you," I snapped. "You have never burned your hair in front of your entire chemistry class, have you? Angel will never let me live this down."

"Angel Rivera?" Mom asked.

"Who else?"

"I'm sure she wouldn't tease you—"

I laughed, a little too loud. The blue-haired woman looked up to glare at me. "You don't know Angel," I told Mom.

"I'm sure if you try, you two can get along," Mom said.

Was it a rule that mothers had to believe everyone could get along if they tried? I could *try* to get along with a grizzly bear, but chances are it would still eat me.

"I will never get along with Angel Rivera," I said.

"You should be nice."

"Why?"

Mom didn't say anything else. She picked up a magazine and became engrossed in an article about perfect piecrusts.

Something weird was going on with her. I had never seen her interested in baking anything in my life.

After a while, a cute guy with blond curls stepped into the room. "Libby Fawcett?" he asked.

I put down the book I'd been hiding behind and stood. "That's me," I mumbled.

The guy's eyes widened when he saw my hair. "What happened?" He put an arm around my shoulder and steered me toward the sinks along the back wall.

"Chemistry class is very dangerous," I told him.

He nodded as I hopped into the black vinyl chair in front of a sink. "Oh, I remember that. I almost blew up my chemistry lab."

"You did not," I said as he began to wash my hair.

He grinned. "You're right, I'm just trying to make you feel better. Did it work?"

It hadn't, but I lied and said it had. He chatted nonstop as he worked on my hair, doing whatever he could so I wouldn't look hideous. It couldn't get much worse than it already was and I didn't dare look in the mirror as the brown strands tumbled to the floor.

It felt like hours had passed when the cute stylist asked, "Are you ready to see the new you?"

I took a deep breath.

He spun the chair around so that I faced the mirror and saw—

A stranger.

As I looked closer, I saw that the girl in the mirror had my features, but the hair . . . The hair on *her* head wasn't frizzy and burned in one spot. It was sleek, shining, and cropped really short, but with a slightly messy look to it and long bangs swept to one side. *She* looked like she could have stepped out of a magazine. No way was I looking at myself.

"Do you like it?" The stylist stood behind me, squeezing my shoulders. His smile was so wide, his head should have split open.

I nodded, still staring at my reflection.

"The other kids in your class won't even remember your burned hair," he assured me as he helped me out of the chair. He gave me a hug before sending me back to the front of the salon.

Mom, with slightly shorter hair, was waiting for me with a new magazine in her hands. She jumped up when she saw me.

"Libby! Wow! You look . . . amazing!"

I tilted my head but my hair was too short to hide behind now. I felt naked and exposed.

"Look at you!" Mom continued, reaching out to run a

hand over my hair. "That cut looks great. You've never had it this short before."

Mom prattled on, not noticing that I hadn't said anything, as she paid the receptionist and we walked out to the car. The wind felt strange on my bare neck.

I sat in the passenger seat, staring silently out the window.

Mom realized I was still quiet and turned to me, one hand on the key in the ignition. "What's wrong?"

A tear slipped down my cheek and then, before I could stop myself, I was sobbing and my shoulders were shaking.

"Libby!" Mom exclaimed. She reached over to pull me into a hug over the console between our seats. "Don't worry, hair grows back. And now it looks terrific!"

I wasn't crying over my hair, though I didn't tell her that. I was crying because it had finally sunk in that I really had burned my hair in chemistry class. In front of Angel. In front of *Seth*. I could never, ever go back to school again. The Internet would be my only contact with the outside world for the rest of my life.

When we got home from the salon, I locked myself in my room and sat down at my computer. I wanted to get out all my thoughts about "the incident," but I did *not* want to talk to anyone.

I used to keep one of those little paper diaries with a cheap lock when I was a kid, but I could never keep it up. So, I found a website that offered free online blogs with password protection. "Share your thoughts with the world, or keep your secrets private with our password system!" the site bragged on its homepage.

I filled in the registration form, and two minutes later an email appeared in my inbox with the subject line "Welcome to your online diary!" The email explained how to lock my entries, and it listed my username and password at the bottom. I signed into my new blog account, set the password-protection filter, and clicked the link to start a new entry.

SOMETHING TO BLOG ABOUT

● ABOUT
● RECENT POSTS
● SEPTEMBER
GIRL ON FIRE
UNIVERSE: 1;
LIBBY: 0

The worst part of this whole ordeal is not Angel's ridicule, which I know is inevitable, but the fact that now I truly have no future with Seth.

Who am I kidding? I never had a chance with him even before this happened. Why would he ever take a second look at me (other than to laugh at my idiocy) when he has Angel hanging all over him?

Now he'll always think of me as the human barbecue from sophomore year chemistry. I can never look him in the eye after this.

It's not just my hair. It's the fact that the whole horrible incident happened—to me. Is there anyone else in the history of the world who has ever burned her hair in chemistry class? No. And do you know why? Because things like this only happen to Libby Fawcett. Isn't it time the universe picked on someone else for a change?

20

KEISHA FOUND ME LYING ON MY BED AFTER she got out of school. I was in disguise in a hoodie, two sizes too big, with the hood pulled up over my head. My black cat, Homer, had cuddled up next to me, purring away.

"Hey, Libs," Keisha said as she bounced onto the edge of my bed. "How are ya?"

I looked at her, with her nice, un-burned hair. Keisha's hair stuck out from her head in full, black curls, with a big green flower barrette holding it back on one side.

I pulled the strings of my hood tight around my face.

"It can't be that bad," Keisha said. "Let me see."

"No way," I said.

"Don't make me kick your butt," Keisha threatened. "I'm not leaving until I see the damage."

Nice choice of words, Keish. I sighed and then pushed the hood down to reveal my short hair.

Keisha bopped me with a pillow. "Why are you hiding? You should *thank* that Bunsen burner."

"I liked my hair the way it was. Boring, invisible. Like me."

"It'll grow back," Keisha pointed out.

I rolled over to bury my face in my pillow. I thought about Seth and cringed. "Did Seth laugh?" I mumbled, my face still in the pillow.

"What? I don't speak Pillow," Keisha said.

I lifted my head and scowled. "Did Seth laugh?"

"I don't know. Angel did, of course, but then Ms. Hoover made us get back to work. I didn't see what Seth was doing."

I let out a long breath and groaned. "He laughed, I'm sure. The whole school is laughing at me by now. There is no way I'm ever going back."

"Seth is, like, the nicest guy in school," Keisha said. "He didn't even laugh that time you slipped on that puddle of water in the cafeteria and spilled your lunch all over yourself. Even *I* had a hard time not cracking up over that. And as for everyone else, I'll kick their butts if they mess with you." Keisha always thought a good butt-kicking could solve everything. "Don't worry. Everyone will forget about this."

"When?" I challenged her. But Keisha didn't have an answer for that.

After she left, Roger instant messaged me.

ZeppelinGuy: Hey, Smokey.

Libtastic0802: Ha-ha.

ZeppelinGuy: Sorry. So how are you? Bald?

Libtastic0802: Yes, Roger. I went home and SHAVED ALL MY HAIR OFF.

ZeppelinGuy: I could shave mine, too, if you want. You know, to show support.

Libtastic0802: Your head is too lumpy for that to look good.

ZeppelinGuy: Only because you hit me so many times when we were kids with that stupid dump truck.

Libtastic0802: Don't mess with my dump truck. It was better than any you ever had.

ZeppelinGuy: You wish.

Libtastic0802: Keisha came over earlier to make me feel better.

ZeppelinGuy: Did Keisha say anything about me?

Libtastic0802: Uh, no. Why would she say anything about you?

ZeppelinGuy: Never mind. I have to go eat dinner.

ZeppelinGuy signed off.

SOMETHING TO BLOG ABOUT

● ABOUT
● RECENT POSTS
● SEPTEMBER
GIRL ON FIRE
UNIVERSE: 1;
LIBBY: 0
SO VERY TEMPTED

FRIDAY, SEPTEMBER 28, 9:37 PM
SO VERY TEMPTED

Mom is so unfair. She actually forced me to go back to school after all the trauma I went through yesterday.

People told me all day how great my hair looked. But I could tell that everyone knew what happened. Most of them at least *tried* not to laugh right in my face.

I had hoped to avoid Angel as long as I could, but she caught me in the girls' room this morning. She tossed her long black hair over her shoulder and said, "Well, I suppose it isn't the hairdresser's fault that there wasn't anything good to work with."

Her clones, Tara Wrigley and Kim Watson, laughed as I pushed past them and out the door.

Would cramming Angel's head into the toilet be grounds for suspension?

24

I WOKE SATURDAY MORNING JUST AFTER
sunrise to get dressed and head out to the track at school.
I always ran a few laps on Saturday mornings to clear my
head and keep in shape during the off-season. I ran for the
school's track team in the spring. Somehow, despite being
ridiculously clumsy, everything worked exactly as it was
supposed to when I ran. I didn't worry about what my arms
and legs were doing, or if I was about to fall flat on my face
when I jumped a hurdle. I just ran.

The track was empty, as usual. The walk to school had
warmed up my muscles, and then I had a good stretch
before starting my run.

I crouched down at the starting line, pretending I was
getting ready for a track meet. I imagined my competitors
on either side of me, their faces creased in concentration.

At the sound of the imaginary gun in my head, I took off, extending my legs as far as I could with each stride. The wind whistled past my ears as I followed the curve in the track and my now too-short-for-a-ponytail hair slapped against my head. I jumped the first hurdle easily and headed toward the second.

Images from Thursday flashed into my head as I ran. I remembered the look of horror on Keisha's and Roger's faces in class. The sounds of my classmates laughing as I left the room. My crying in the car after the haircut.

And I imagined Seth laughing along with the others after "the incident." He probably knew I existed now, but not in the way I had hoped.

I was so focused on the images in my head and the pace of my run that I didn't notice the hurdle I was coming up on was slightly higher than I was used to.

I was nearly on top of it before I realized that I wasn't prepared to jump it. I tried to stop, but it was too late. My arms swung wildly as I tried to regain my balance, but I fell forward onto the wooden hurdle.

Rolling over on the asphalt, I groaned at the pain searing through my palms and knees.

I heard footsteps moving quickly across the track toward me and a voice said, "Are you okay?"

Please no, I thought, squeezing my eyes shut. Anyone but him.

"I'm fine," I answered after a moment. Actually, I was anything but fine. Once again, I had made a complete idiot of myself in front of Seth. I sat up, brushing the bits of rock and dirt from my palms.

"For a minute there I thought you were going to jump it," he said.

Seth offered his hand to help me stand. My skin exploded into tingles when I slipped my hand in his.

"Are you sure you're all right? Here, let me look at those scratches."

He turned my hands over, holding them gently while he looked at my wounds. I felt heat rising from my neck and face, and I looked away to hide my blush.

"I'm okay," I told him. "Just minor scrapes." I pulled my hands from his grasp and hobbled to the bleachers, where I had left my towel and water bottle. My bloody left knee ached.

"Your run looked really good," Seth said, following me. "You know, until the end."

"Thanks." I turned away and took a long drink of water to avoid looking at him.

"How's your hair?" Seth asked.

I nearly choked on my mouthful of water. "Fine. It's fine."

He had his hands in the pockets of his usual brown corduroy jacket as he leaned over the fence. "You know everyone in school calls you Smokey now, right?"

Great. I was going to kill Roger if he was the one who started that.

I couldn't look at Seth for fear that I'd probably start crying. "Funny," I mumbled.

"It's kind of cute," he said. "And never let it be said that you don't know how to get attention."

He was poking fun at me, but I couldn't take it. I may have burned my hair, but I still had my pride.

Slinging my towel over my shoulder, I said, "I have to go."

Seth grabbed my arm. "Wait, I'm sorry. I was just joking around."

Tears formed at the corners of my eyes. Suck it up, I told myself. You don't cry in front of people, remember? The last time I had cried in front of anyone other than my mom was in the third grade when I fell off the jungle gym on the school playground. I wasn't seriously hurt, but I bruised my hip and started crying right in front of a boy named Erik—the meanest kid in our class. He called me Cribby for the rest of the year—short for Crybaby Libby.

I would not be Cribby in front of Seth. I bit my lip hard, but that just made my eyes tear up even more. Pretending to be wiping away sweat, I rubbed at my face with my towel.

"What are you doing here so early anyway?" I asked.

Seth shrugged. "Sometimes I like getting up before everyone else." He bent over and leaned all his weight on the fence, letting his hair hang down in his face.

"Hey, how are you doing in chemistry?" he asked as he straightened. "I mean, besides the burning your hair part. How are your grades?"

I had no hope for a future as a chemist, but he didn't need to know that, so I just said, "I'm doing okay."

"Okay enough to tutor me?"

Alone with Seth Jacobs for tutoring sessions? If that were the case, I'd memorize my *entire* chemistry book.

"Are you sure you really want my help?" I asked. "It may be dangerous to your health. Won't Janet help you?" (Janet Li probably wasn't on the verge of an F.)

"Janet doesn't like me very much," Seth admitted. "She said I spend too much time flirting with Angel."

A sharp pain shot through my heart at those words. "Then get Angel to help you."

Seth snorted. "Angel is about as clueless in chemistry as I am. I have to get help from someone, and you seemed really smart that time we did that project in English. *Animal Farm*, remember? You drew that cool pig. Anyway, my dad said it's either get a passing grade or lose my car and ride the bus to school for the rest of the year!"

Well, of course I couldn't force Seth to ride the bus!

I ignored that little voice in my head that reminded me of my last chemistry quiz. Underneath the D minus, Ms. Hoover had written, "Please see me." That was never a good thing.

"I'd be happy to help you out."

He gave me one of his amazing smiles. "Great. I'll call you and we can set things up."

"My number's in the phone book," I told him. "Under Maura Fawcett. That's my mom. Maura."

"Thanks, Libby. This really means a lot."

As he walked away, that voice in my head screeched that I was out of my mind. I had volunteered to help the guy of my dreams attempt to pass a subject that might as well have been Latin. My help was likely to make him lose his car forever.

There was only one logical option: I had to find a tutor for myself so I could tutor Seth.

• • •

I was such an idiot. I should have set an exact time for Seth to call.

I had plans with Keisha and Roger that night to see a new movie we'd been talking about ever since we saw the trailer online. I'd been looking forward to it—up until my meeting with Seth. Suddenly, I wanted nothing more than to stay home and sit by the phone.

"This is not just some ordinary guy!" I shrieked into the phone at Keisha. "This is Seth Jacobs, the guy I have loved for two years. I *cannot* miss his call!"

"Libby, listen to me carefully," Keisha said. "If you try to bail on your friends for a *guy*, I will have reasonable cause to kick your scrawny white butt. Your mom knows how to take a message. We'll pick you up at eight. Be ready."

I was reluctantly ready when Roger pulled into the parking lot in front of my apartment building and beeped the horn. I glanced at the phone one last time before I walked out the door, willing it to ring at that moment so I could rush back to answer it. But it stayed silent.

"He's going to call, isn't he?" I asked as the opening credits started to roll. I looked at Roger. "You're a guy. Tell me that he'll call."

Roger held up his hands. "I can't predict what Seth

Jacobs may or may not do. Being male doesn't make me a mind reader."

"What good are *you* then?" I grumbled, crossing my arms over my chest.

"Shh!" someone behind us in the darkened theater hissed.

"I'm sure he'll call," Roger said. "He said he needed your help."

"Then why hasn't he called already?"

"Guys don't call the very same day," Keisha informed me as she munched on the Raisinettes Roger had bought for her. "They take their time. You'll only drive yourself completely crazy if you expect a call so soon. And while we're on this topic, why are *you* tutoring someone in chemistry anyway?"

"Thanks for the vote of confidence. It's nice to know my friends think I'm dumb."

"I did *not* say anything about you being dumb," Keisha snapped. "I'm your lab partner, and I know what your test scores look like. I also happen to know how little you are interested in chemistry. So please excuse me if hearing that you're tutoring someone else takes me by surprise. Anyway, I could tutor him if you want."

"No way," I told her. "You have to tutor *me* so I can tutor *him*."

"This tutoring thing sounds really complicated," Roger said.

"Shh!" someone hissed again.

It was no use trying to focus on the movie. Seth Jacobs wanted *me* to spend time with *him* for private tutoring sessions. And I'd seen enough teen movies to know that "tutoring" didn't always mean *tutoring*.

SUNDAY, SEPTEMBER 30, 1:22 PM
MY BEST FRIEND, THE NUTCASE

Sometimes I think Keisha is a mental case waiting to be unleashed.

She's my best friend and I love her, but all those threats must be the early signs of psychotic behavior. Why else would a seemingly normal person threaten to kick the butt of the scrawny guy behind the movie snack counter because he wouldn't give her a fourth refill on her Coke?

Luckily, I happened to have a few Raisinettes left in the bottom of my box and was able to distract her with those. It's either a mental problem or chronic low blood sugar. I'm not sure which.

- ABOUT
- RECENT POSTS
- SEPTEMBER
GIRL ON FIRE

UNIVERSE: 1;
LIBBY: 0

SO VERY TEMPTED

MY BEST FRIEND,
THE NUTCASE

34

THE PHONE RANG JUST AS MOM AND I SAT down for a lunch of grilled cheese sandwiches on Sunday. We had both been racing each other to the phone the last few weeks—I had no idea who Mom was so eager to hear from all of a sudden—but this time my foot caught on my chair leg as I tried to stand up, and I ended up sprawled on the kitchen floor while Mom grabbed the phone. "Hello?" She listened for a moment, then held the phone toward me, her eyebrows raised.

"It's a boy," she whispered as I picked myself up from the floor.

My hands shook as I reached for the receiver and swallowed the chunk of grilled cheese in my mouth.

"Hello?"

"Hi, Smokey."

Suddenly that nickname didn't sound so bad.

"Hi." Cradling the phone on my shoulder, I stretched the cord as far as it would go so I wouldn't have to talk to Seth in front of my mother. "Um, how are you?"

Could I have sounded any more like a dork?

"I'm good," Seth answered. "So you'll still tutor me, right?"

As if there was any way I'd miss out on an opportunity to spend private time with a guy who looked like Seth.

"Of course I will," I said, twisting the phone cord around my fingers. I hoped I didn't sound too eager. I didn't want him to think I was a loser with nothing else to do *or* that I was overly excited about chemistry.

"Great," Seth said. "How's tomorrow after school? We can meet in the library."

"Right, the library. Perfect."

"You're awesome, Libby. I'll be eternally grateful to you if we manage to pull my grades up."

So grateful that he might kiss me? I thought to myself.

I skipped back to the kitchen to hang up the phone.

"Who was that?" Mom asked, eyeing me over the remaining half of her sandwich.

"Just a guy," I said as I sat down. Too excited to eat, I pushed my plate away.

"What's this about the library?"

"You were listening to my phone call?" I asked.

"This apartment isn't very big. I couldn't help hearing you speak. Who is this guy? Do I know him?"

"Seth Jacobs." Saying his name sent shivers throughout my body.

"That guy you've been drooling over since the eighth grade?"

I scowled across the table at her. "Do you know all my secrets?"

"Again, this apartment isn't very big. You're not exactly quiet when Keisha sleeps over."

I could see that I'd have to be more careful of what I said when I was home. Did the neighbors know all about my obsession as well?

"Yes, that Seth," I said. "I'm tutoring him in chemistry."

"*You're* tutoring someone in chemistry?" Mom asked, raising one eyebrow.

"Why does everyone keep saying that?"

"Libby, no offense, but you are my daughter and you inherited my scientific brain. Which means you don't have one. How are you supposed to teach someone something that you can't understand?"

"I already have that covered. Keisha's tutoring me, then I'm tutoring Seth."

"And Keisha can't tutor Seth because . . . ?"

"Because *I* like Seth!" I exclaimed. "And if I tutor him, that means I get time alone with him."

Mom nodded slowly. "Ah, I see. You don't want to tutor Seth, you want to *tutor* Seth. Very clever."

I smiled. "Thank you."

Mom got up to clear the table. "I must warn you, however, that if I find out he's *tutoring* you in *certain* extracurricular activities, I will be forced to kill him."

ZeppelinGuy: How do you make a girl like you?

Libtastic0802: Hmm, let me think. My girl-attracting moves are a bit rusty.

ZeppelinGuy: Ha-ha, dork. How do you get a person of an undefined gender to like you?

Libtastic0802: I'm trying to study chemistry right now. I have to know this stuff before tomorrow afternoon.

ZeppelinGuy: I listened to you babble about Seth for two hours last night. You can give me five minutes.

Libtastic0802: Fine. Go ahead. I'm listening. Er, reading.

ZeppelinGuy: I like someone, but she doesn't know. How do I go about telling her?

Libtastic0802: How about, "I like you. Wanna go out Friday night?"

ZeppelinGuy: Yeah, and why is it that you can't say that to Seth?

Libtastic0802: We're talking about you, remember?

ZeppelinGuy: Then tell me what to do.

Libtastic0802: I don't know. I can't tell you what to do when I don't even know who she is.

ZeppelinGuy: Why does that make a difference?

Libtastic0802: Because you can't just use the same moves on one girl that you would use on another. Everyone likes different things.

ZeppelinGuy: If I tell you, you have to promise you will never say a word.

Libtastic0802: Promise.

ZeppelinGuy: Swear it on Homer's life.

Libtastic0802: I will not involve my cat in this.

ZeppelinGuy: Fine. It's Keisha.

Libtastic0802: Keisha who?

ZeppelinGuy: KEISHA JONES, nitwit.

Libtastic0802: You like Keisha?!

ZeppelinGuy: YES. But you canNOT say a word. Remember?

Libtastic0802: Fine. But don't blame me if it happens to slip out. You know how I am sometimes.

ZeppelinGuy: I knew I should have asked someone else.

Libtastic0802: Keisha is not like most girls. She's cynical, she's sarcastic. She's . . . capable of causing bodily harm. Are you sure you want to go out with her?

ZeppelinGuy: Just tell me what to do.

Libtastic0802: I don't know . . . Do something unexpected. Catch her off guard.

ZeppelinGuy: Hmm.

Libtastic0802: What?

ZeppelinGuy: Gotta go.

Libtastic0802: Wait! WHAT??

ZeppelinGuy signed off.

SOMETHING TO BLOG ABOUT

I cannot focus on anything in any of my classes today. This afternoon Seth and I begin our tutoring.

As if it isn't bad enough that I'm stressing over the first session and the fact that one of my best friends is in love with my other best friend, Angel tripped me in the hall after second period this morning. She tried to act as though it was an accident, but it *so* was not. One minute I'm walking and the path in front of me is as clear as it can get in the hall of a high school, and the next minute Angel's backpack is on the floor right in front of me. I tried to hop over it, but she caught me off guard and I landed on my face, toppling Miguel Sanchez on my way down. Unfortunately, he was carrying his trumpet case. Which I also happened to land on.

• ABOUT
• RECENT POSTS
• SEPTEMBER
• OCTOBER
MY RIBS REALLY HURT

41

DURING OUR LUNCH PERIOD, I FORCED KEISHA to write out a cheat sheet of things I should know from the first chapter of my chemistry book. She grudgingly agreed to give me mini-tutoring sessions in homeroom each morning, which would give me fifteen minutes a day to learn everything I needed to know about chemistry.

"I don't understand why I can't tutor both you *and* Seth in the afternoon," Keisha said as she wrote out some formulas in my notebook.

"Because," I explained, my patience wearing thin, "I do not want you around while I'm spending time with Seth. What if he gets the desire to kiss me, but is too embarrassed to do it in front of someone else? Do you want to be responsible for Seth Jacobs *not* kissing me?"

"Okay, forget I asked," Keisha said, rolling her eyes.

While Keisha was busy writing out what I needed to know, I joined Roger in the lunch line and tried to get him to tell me what he planned to do about his crush on Keisha.

"Come on," I whispered, shaking his arm back and forth. "What are you up to? I'm your blood, you *have* to tell me."

"The football team is really looking good this year, isn't it?" Roger asked, shooting me a smirk.

"That is *so* not an answer," I told him. But Roger's lips were sealed tight.

I never realized just how many people actually stayed after school in the library. Several tables were already occupied by students scribbling notes and going through stacks of books. Two cheerleaders sat in the magazine section filling out a quiz in *Seventeen*. I knew they were doing the quiz because one was reading the questions out loud for the other to answer. Ms. Taylor, the librarian, had to go tell them to use their "library voices" several times. I also saw six or seven students at the computers. Most seemed to be typing papers, but one kid was clearly checking his email and another was looking at photos of women's feet in *really* high heels.

Didn't these people have anything better to do than sit in

the library after school? And didn't that foot-fetish kid have a computer at home where he could look at that stuff?

Seth sat at a table near the biographies. This was a major disappointment for me because everyone knew that the make-out stacks were back in the world history section.

"I was worried that you might have changed your mind," Seth told me.

"Of course not," I said, sitting down next to him. "Ready to study some chemistry?"

Seth made a face but opened his textbook. He turned to chapter four, which we were currently working on in class.

I sneaked a glance at the notes Keisha had made. "Maybe we should start at the beginning. To make sure you understand the basics." I didn't mention that I needed to make sure *I* understood the basics, as well.

"Okay," Seth agreed.

We read from the first chapter for a while (in low tones to avoid the wrath of Ms. Taylor) and discussed the bolded definitions within the text. I watched Seth make notes in his small, blocky print. I liked the way he held his pencil, grasping it carefully as if he was afraid it would break. I imagined him holding me like that, thinking I was so precious I might shatter from his touch.

Seth put his pencil down and rubbed his eyes. "I'll never get this. I write it down, but I still have no clue what anything means."

I wanted to reach out to pat his hand, but I resisted the urge, thinking that might be a little TV-mom-ish. Instead, I stuck my hands under my legs.

"You'll get it," I told him. "We only just started."

Seth gave me a half-smile. "Thanks for the vote of confidence. I hope I don't let you down."

"Just do your best," I said. Okay, now *that* really was TV-mom-ish. I should have just kept my mouth shut, smiled a little, and tried to look cute.

Seth bent back over his textbook, reading a paragraph about the periodic table, his shaggy hair falling over his face. I wanted to reach up and brush his hair out of his eyes and then pull his face to mine. It was a good thing I was still sitting on my hands.

SOMETHING TO BLOG ABOUT

● ABOUT
● RECENT POSTS
● SEPTEMBER
● OCTOBER

MY RIBS REALLY HURT

KEEPING SECRETS IS HARD WORK

MONDAY, OCTOBER 1, 4:22 PM
KEEPING SECRETS IS HARD WORK

How could Roger have put such a huge burden on me—his favorite cousin in the entire world? He knows I have problems keeping secrets. In the eighth grade, he told me that he had a crush on our English teacher and made me swear not to tell anyone. It only took two days before that little bit of news slipped out and soon everyone in school knew about it. He didn't talk to me for a month. Kids teased him for the rest of the year.

All day, I had to stop myself from telling Keisha that Roger liked her. I could feel the words right there on the end of my tongue, just begging for me to let them out.

46

"SO HOW DID THE *TUTORING* GO?" MOM
asked when she got home.

"The tutoring went fine," I said. "We read most of the
first chapter of our book and talked about the periodic
table."

"Sounds very romantic."

I stuck my tongue out at her back as she walked into the
kitchen. What did she know about romance anyway? She
never had a relationship last longer than three dates. Other
than with my dad.

Okay, so maybe chemistry didn't exactly conjure up
images of candlelit dinners or moonlit walks on the beach,
but everyone has to start somewhere. All I had to do was
help Seth with chemistry and then he'd be so grateful he'd

tell me that he would never have passed the class without me. And then he would look into my eyes and realize they were the exact shade of brown as his jacket and know it was a sign that we were meant to be. And he'd fall madly in love with me. We'd tell our grandchildren how our romance began when I burned my hair. And everyone would toast us at our fiftieth wedding anniversary, and when someone asked how our love survived all those years, we'd look at each other and laugh and say, "Chemistry."

It could happen.

The phone rang and both Mom and I dashed to answer it. I reached it first.

"Hello?" I said into the receiver, hoping it was Keisha so I could tell her all about my afternoon with Seth.

"Oh, hello," said a deep voice I didn't recognize. "May I speak with Maura?"

"Let me check if she's gotten home yet. Who should I say is speaking?" I asked. Mom hated telemarketers—with a fiery passion—so I tried to save them from her fury.

"This is Manny," the man said. "I'm a . . . friend."

I frowned as I held the phone out to my mom. "Manny?" I said.

Mom's face turned white for a moment, then reddened.

She snatched the phone from my hands, stretched the phone cord down the hall and into her room, and shut the door behind her.

I hesitated a moment, thinking how much trouble I'd be in if Mom caught me snooping. Then I tiptoed to the door and pressed my ear against the wood. I couldn't hear anything over my own breathing, so I held my breath.

"I told you not to call until later," Mom said. She didn't sound angry. She spoke in a soft voice I'd never heard her use before. "I miss you, too . . . No, not . . . I don't . . . Maybe after . . ."

I was missing key words! I tried to press my ear closer to the door.

"Yes, tomorrow," Mom was saying. "I'll see you at . . ."

I couldn't hear what she said after that, but it was clear that Mom was ending the conversation. I hurried back to the kitchen, stubbing my toe on the refrigerator on the way in. I had to bite down hard on my lip to keep from muttering a string of curses.

Mom sauntered into the kitchen like nothing was wrong. She hung up the phone and then opened the cabinet by the stove.

"What do you want for dinner?" she asked.

"Who's Manny?" I countered.

"Who?" She inspected a can of tomatoes.

"The guy who was on the phone, like, five seconds ago."

"Oh." Mom shrugged. "Just a friend from work."

I watched as her neck reddened, just like mine always did when I was embarrassed or nervous or when I wasn't telling the truth.

I thought about her nights out over the last few months and her happy humming as she did chores. I suddenly realized what it all meant. I couldn't believe I hadn't figured it out before.

"Mom," I said, leaning against the counter and crossing my arms over my chest, "are you *dating* someone?"

She didn't answer, but I knew I had guessed correctly because she looked really uncomfortable.

"So that's where you've been going!" I exclaimed. "It's this Manny, right? Who is he? What does he do? Why haven't you mentioned him? Why haven't I met him?"

"He's a lawyer, and whether or not I'm dating anyone is my own concern," Mom told me. She turned her back to me as she started to prepare our dinner. "I'm the mother here, remember?"

"Yes, but as your daughter, I have a right to know about the man in your life. You know all about my crush on Seth."

"He's just a gentleman I've been going out with."

"What are you, seventy?" I asked. "Have you made out yet?"

"Elizabeth!" Mom's shoulders shook as if she were trying hard not to laugh.

"So you *have* made out, huh?" I loved teasing my mother. Finally, after fifteen years, I had something to use against her. For once she was the dreamy-eyed girl drooling over a boy and I got to be the mature one.

"I want to meet him." I needed to see this guy for myself, to find out whether or not he was good enough for my mom.

"You will," Mom said. "When I'm ready."

"I've met other guys you've gone out with before," I pointed out.

"I really like Manny, but I want to make sure things are going to last a while before I introduce him to you," Mom said.

I sighed. "That's fair, I guess. How long have you been seeing him?"

"A few months."

"Months!" I exclaimed. "How many?"

"Seven."

"Seven months! Mom, that's practically forever! Aren't you sure yet?"

"When you get older, you realize seven months isn't that long at all," she told me. She pulled some pots out of the cabinet and set them on the stove. "You'll meet him, I promise."

"Fine," I said. "But in the meantime, I want you home by ten each night and don't spend all of your time on the phone when you should be studying."

Mom swatted at me as I hurried out of the room.

NotUrDreamGrrl: How did the tutoring go?

Libtastic0802: GREAT. Keisha, it was the best afternoon I've ever spent at school. We talked, we studied, and he smiled at me A LOT. I sat right next to him for an HOUR.

NotUrDreamGrrl: So you think this tutoring thing will work out then?

Libtastic0802: Of course. As long as you can go over things with me in the mornings, I'll have no problem going over them with Seth in the afternoons.

NotUrDreamGrrl: The offer still stands to tutor both of you at the same time.

Libtastic0802: NO. Don't ever suggest that again.

NotUrDreamGrrl: Fine, fine. Hey, did Roger seem like he was acting weird today?

Libtastic0802: No, I don't know what you're talking about. He seemed like the same old Roger to me.

NotUrDreamGrrl: He just seemed like he wasn't talking to me like he usually does. Did I do anything to make him mad?

Libtastic0802: Not that I know of.

NotUrDreamGrrl: Maybe I'm imagining things.

Libtastic0802: You are. I gotta go. I just got the new issue of *Seventeen*.

Libtastic0802 signed off.

SOMETHING TO BLOG ABOUT

MONDAY, OCTOBER 1, 7:22 PM
MYSTERY MAN

I cannot believe my mother. She knows all of my secrets, but she won't tell me any of hers. SO NOT FAIR!

I don't know why I didn't figure out that she was dating someone sooner. I mean, I've known her for fifteen years. She shouldn't be able to keep things like this from me without my realizing it.

Who is this Manny???

WHEN WE ARRIVED AT SCHOOL THAT
morning, Keisha and I noticed a group of kids standing by
her locker, but we couldn't see what was going on.

"Probably Angel and some guy again," Keisha muttered.
Angel's locker was next to Keisha's and she often arrived
there to find Angel making out with her boyfriend of the
day. What exactly did you say in a situation like that? In
Keisha's case it was, "Get away from my locker before I kick
your butt."

We pushed through the crowd and found out that it
wasn't Angel everyone was gaping at, but she was in the
crowd, too. She turned to us as we approached.

"Aw, how sweet," Angel cooed. "Did your girlfriend
Elizabeth send you flowers, Keisha? You know, I always had
a feeling about you two."

"Get out of my way." Keisha pushed Angel aside, knocking her back into the lockers. I finally got a clear view of what had everyone's attention.

A giant arrangement of pink and white carnations sat atop a white plastic pedestal in front of Keisha's locker. The heart-shaped arrangement had a center of six red roses.

"*What* is *that?*" Keisha asked. From the look on her face, the flowers might as well have been an arrangement of decapitated mice instead.

I dug through the flowers until I found a pink card. "'Even this isn't as big as my love for you,'" I read out loud. "No signature."

Keisha spun around and glared at Angel. "Is this your idea of a joke?"

Angel made a snorting noise. "I have better things to spend my money on than that hideous thing." She waved her fingers at us and disappeared down the hallway.

I stared at the flowers, trying to keep my face from showing what I was thinking—I knew who had sent the flowers. And I couldn't wait to smack him over the head.

Keisha grunted as she dragged the flowers away from her locker. "This thing weighs a ton! How did someone get it in here—with a forklift? Can you believe someone thought that—" Keisha nodded at the beast of a flower arrangement as she opened her locker. "—*this* might actually be a good idea? Anyone who wants to express their undying love for me should know me well enough to understand that this is *not* the way to my heart."

I had to say something. I couldn't let Keisha rant on about how much she hated the gift, not when I knew who her admirer was.

"I think it's really sweet," I blurted out. "I mean, I would love it if a guy bought me flowers."

"*Flowers*, maybe," Keisha said. "But not the King of All Things Hideous." She glared at the arrangement. "Just how am I supposed to take that home?"

"But look!" I tried to think of something to change Keisha's mind. "Pink and red! Those—those are the colors of love! This guy must *love* you, Keisha."

"You can have the flowers then. Now he loves you."

Considering this was my cousin we were talking about, that was gross.

Ms. Wilkins, the assistant principal, came on the intercom system to read the morning announcements as we sat down in homeroom. After the usual details about the day's lunch and upcoming club and athletic events, she said, "Would the owner of the large, um, *bouquet* of flowers in the south hall please move it to the front office? It is interfering with movement through that area. Thank you."

Keisha snapped her history book shut and sprang from her seat. She muttered under her breath as she stomped out of the room.

I had to find Roger. I raced out of homeroom, hoping to catch him before the bell rang.

"Hey," said a voice near my ear.

Seth stood at my side. My heart felt as if it had skipped twenty beats.

"We still on for this afternoon?" he asked.

I nodded. "Yes, of course. Well, unless you have something else you need to do."

"No, I just wanted to make sure you weren't ready to give up on me already," he said.

"No way. I promised to help."

He stuffed his hands into his pockets and leaned against the wall. "I'm sure you have better things to do than waste all your time with me."

Any time with Seth was time not wasted.

I shook my head. "Nah, I don't have anything pressing

to do in the afternoons this time of year, since track isn't in season. I'm all yours."

Angel and her friend Tara chose that very moment to walk by in all their gorgeousness. "Hi, Seth," they said in unison, flashing bright smiles.

Seth nodded to them as they passed and called out, "Hey, Angel, wait up." He smiled at me one last time and said, "See you," before heading down the hall after her.

Angel looked over her shoulder at me, smiling triumphantly.

Suddenly I remembered I had to find Roger right away.

This was a matter of *love* and *hate*, namely Roger's love of Keisha and Keisha's hate of all things floral.

I raced down the hall, almost tripping Miguel Sanchez, who was not carrying his trumpet this time, thankfully, but who did shoot me a nasty look when he regained his balance.

I found Roger walking out of his homeroom, talking to two guys he hung out with sometimes.

I grabbed his arm. "I have to talk to you."

"I can't *believe* this!" a voice screeched behind us.

I squeezed my eyes shut. *Go away, go away!*

But when I opened my eyes, Keisha was still there,

shoving papers into her backpack as she grumbled to herself. How had she gotten down the hall so quickly? The front office was all the way at the other end of the building. I should have had plenty of time to warn Roger.

"What is it?" Roger asked, shrugging out of my grasp.

"Have you seen that hideous thing someone planted in front of my locker?" Keisha asked. "First I had to get it out of the way just so I could get to my locker. Then I had to hunt down the janitor during homeroom to help me move it to the office. Now Ms. Wilkins says I *have* to take it home this afternoon! I was going to leave it there because maybe the school could use some craptastic flower arrangement, since I certainly have no desire to keep it, but no! Ms. Wilkins says if I try to leave it, she'll call my mom this afternoon and insist she come pick it up."

I watched Roger's face as Keisha rambled on, biting my lip hard. He looked absolutely heartbroken. He didn't say a word, but I saw how tight his hands gripped the edges of his math book.

Why couldn't Keisha have stayed away for five seconds more?

"I'll help you with it," I blurted, to stop Keisha from stomping on Roger's heart any further.

"That thing weighs more than you do," Keisha told me.

"I'll help you," Roger said in a weird voice, sounding like he had something stuck in his throat. "I'll meet you after the last bell."

Keisha smiled at him. "Thanks, Rog. Why can't other guys be like you? You'd know better than to send a girl something like that." She waved as she headed off down the hall.

I turned back to Roger. "Rog—"

"Don't, Libby," he said.

"Don't what?"

"Don't try to cheer me up." He slumped back against the wall and stared up at the ceiling. "I had this all figured out. It was going to be so romantic. I'd leave a gift every few days with a clue until she figured out who I am."

"And then she'd kick your butt!" I exclaimed. "If you were doing this for me, it would work exactly as you want it to. But not Keisha." I lowered my voice and tried to explain. "Keisha isn't like other girls. You can't just do the same old things that you would for anyone else."

"What do I do then?"

"Make her think you like all the same dumb things that she does," I said. "But don't send her any more flowers that need their own zip code."

He puffed out his chest. "I can handle it."

I hoped so. Winning Keisha back after sending her that beast of flowers wouldn't be easy.

Seth and I sat one table back from where we sat yesterday—we were moving closer to the make-out stacks. Did that mean he wanted to kiss me—but didn't know how to say so? Maybe we'd just move closer and closer to the make-out stacks in hopes that we'd just end up there one day?

Or had he chosen that table only because the math club occupied the one we'd used before?

"Hey! I was reading the stuff we went over yesterday," Seth told me. "I think I'm starting to get it. I even remembered some of the definitions without looking."

"That's great," I said, trying to sound encouraging.

He smiled. "You're a good teacher. Much better than Ms. Hoover."

I felt my cheeks grow hot. "Thanks."

I needed to thank Keisha later.

We read through the rest of the chapter, although it was hard at times to hear ourselves over the laughing and squealing of the math club. I had no idea what they were doing, but Ms. Taylor had to yell, "Library voices!" at them about a million times before finally threatening to throw them out. Really, who knew the math club could be so exciting they'd cause a disturbance in the library?

After the math club finally settled down again, we were able to focus on our work. Once, when Seth leaned over to ask about a certain formula in the book, his knee touched mine.

It took all I could to not let out a squeal and endure the wrath of Ms. Taylor.

The touch sent a tingle all the way through me.

I vowed to never wash those jeans again.

SOMETHING TO BLOG ABOUT

FRIDAY, OCTOBER 5, 1:47 PM
MY MOM DID MY LAUNDRY!

MOM WASHED MY JEANS!!!

"Sorry," she said when I yelled after finding my jeans in the dryer. "I didn't know smelly jeans were in style now."

Then she rolled her eyes when I explained that *this* particular pair of jeans had touched Seth's. Like she wouldn't do the same thing if she were my age and her jeans had touched that Manny guy's!

KEISHA STOPPED SUDDENLY WHEN SHE walked into the door of our chemistry class. So suddenly that I ran into her, butting my forehead on the back of her head.

"Ow," I said. "What did you do that for?"

But all Keisha said was, "*What* is that on my desk?"

I looked over her shoulder to see what she was talking about.

Hundreds of red hearts were on top of her desk—literally covering every square inch.

Keisha approached the desk slowly, glaring around the room.

"Who did this?" she asked.

The few who were already seated looked at her and shrugged, saying it was like that when they came in. Seth sat in his usual seat in the back, but he was slumped over with his head on his desktop.

Roger appeared at my side. "What's going on?" he asked.

"Like you don't know," I whispered.

He grinned in response.

"How did you do that without anyone seeing?"

"Ms. Hoover doesn't have a class right before this one. I just had to skip history and sneak in here while she was in the teacher's lounge." He flexed his right hand and winced. "My arm is killing me from cutting all those hearts."

Hadn't he ever heard of a crafts store?

Keisha picked some of the hearts off her desk, starting to ball them up, but stopped, staring down at the ones in her hand.

"What is it?" I asked, moving toward her. Small type covered each of the hearts. "'You don't need the police, pal, you need a psychiatrist,'" I read to her.

My mouth dropped open. What was Roger thinking?

"Did a pack of first-graders attack your desk or is that another gift from Elizabeth?" Angel smirked at her own joke.

But Keisha had a smile on her face. Was insulting her really the way to win her heart?

"Something wrong?" Roger asked innocently.

"It's from *Killer Klowns from Outer Space*," Keisha said. She looked at some of the other hearts. "These are all lines from the movie."

Keisha despised romantic, weepy movies, but she loved horror. And *Killer Klowns from Outer Space* was her favorite. Keisha had forced me to watch it ten thousand times because I forced her to watch my favorite romantic comedies.

"He *does* know me," she said softly, her smile widening.

SOMETHING TO BLOG ABOUT

● ABOUT
● RECENT POSTS
● SEPTEMBER
● OCTOBER

Keisha says I am the only dork who leaves a sleepover early to go run. She doesn't understand that running on Saturday mornings is what keeps me semi-sane the rest of the week. Running clears my head.

I didn't expect, however, to arrive home to a sight that not even running could erase from my brain.

I can hear them in the kitchen right now and . . . Ugh, I don't even want to think about it.

AFTER I HAD FINISHED MY RUN AROUND the school's track Saturday morning, during which time I thought about Seth and how his eyes were gray with little green flecks around the center, and I thought a little about Roger and Keisha, I walked back home feeling awake and refreshed. I didn't have any answers as to how to make Seth like me or how to get my two friends together, but I felt good about the day ahead.

I dragged the bag I'd taken to the sleepover at Keisha's the night before up the stairs to our apartment. Outside the door, I could hear the TV on, so I knew Mom was up already.

"Mom, I'm home!" I dropped my bag by the door and walked to the kitchen. "I need a long, hot shower—"

I stopped, frozen in place. Mom sat at the table, also

frozen, a forkful of eggs halfway to her mouth. She wore a short pink satin nightie, one I had seen in her dresser but had never seen her wear.

At the head of the table sat a man, dressed in only a pair of plaid boxer shorts.

Mom dropped her fork onto her plate. "Libby!" she exclaimed. "What—I thought you were at Keisha's."

She looked as if she had been caught spraying graffiti on the walls. She pulled the hem of her nightie down a bit, glancing from me to the man at her side.

My brain screamed, "Look away! Look away!" But I couldn't. I kept staring at my half-naked mother and her half-naked companion, and even though I wanted to barf at the thought that they had spent the night together, I couldn't tear my eyes away from the sight before me.

The man cleared his throat. "Hello, Libby," he said. "I've heard a lot about you." He started to stand, then remembered he was only wearing boxer shorts and decided to stay seated. "I'm Manuel Rivera, but please call me Manny."

That name snapped me out of my stupor. "Rivera? As in *Angel* Rivera?"

He looked at my mother, who shook her head slightly.

He nodded at her and then said to me, "Angel is my daughter."

I couldn't breathe. My chest felt tight. Was my left arm going numb? I knew Angel's dad was single because her mom had died when she was a baby, but I'd never imagined my mother might be dating him. Or doing *more* than just dating him.

"I understand the two of you go to school together," Mr. Rivera said, smiling, clearly oblivious to the heart attack I was having.

I couldn't say a word. I opened my mouth, but nothing came out.

"Libby?" Mom asked. "Are you all right?"

Finally I was able to tear my gaze from the disaster in front of me. I dashed to my room, stumbling, and slammed the door behind me.

My mother was dating the father of my mortal enemy. How *could* she?

I could hear them in the kitchen, cleaning up their dishes and talking in voices too low for me to make out the words. Hopefully Mom was telling Manuel Rivera that she made a mistake and couldn't possibly date him due to his demon-spawn child making her own child's life a living hell.

I heard the sound of the front door closing a few minutes later, and then footsteps moving down the hall toward my room.

"Can I come in?" Mom asked through the door.

"It's a free country," I answered.

Mom opened the door and sat down on the edge of the bed, facing me. She had pulled her robe on over her nightie. I wanted to keep plenty of space between us to keep the Rivera germs from contaminating me.

"I'm so sorry," Mom said. "I didn't mean for you to meet Manny like this. It won't happen again, okay? I explained to Manny how uncomfortable I was when you walked in and we agreed it was for the best."

"Thank God you came to your senses," I cried. "The Riveras are *evil*. It's best to get away from him while you still can." I patted her hand. "Don't worry, you'll meet someone else soon."

Mom blinked at me. "Libby, what are you talking about?"

"You breaking up with Mr. Rivera."

"What? Why would I do that?" Mom looked at me as if I were crazy.

"Because," I explained slowly, "he is *Angel Rivera's* father."

"What goes on at school is between you and Angel," Mom told me. "Manny and I will continue to see each other. I only meant that he won't spend the night over here again so you don't have to come across any more scenes like this morning."

"Mom!" I exclaimed. My outburst startled Homer, who had been sleeping on my pillows. He looked at me and meowed angrily. "You can't betray your daughter for some guy!"

"I am not betraying you," Mom told me, her face reddening. "And he is not just some guy. Manny and I are in love."

I flopped down on my bed, burying my head into the mattress. "I'm not going to win this, am I? You've already gone over to the dark side."

Mom leaned over so that her head rested on my shoulder. "Hey," she said. "You haven't lost me to anything or anyone. I'm still your mother and I always will be. I've just found a man who makes me truly happy and who loves me. Is that so terrible?"

"No," I said, sighing. Geez, she really knew how to lay it on thick to make me feel bad. "But why did you have to pick *him*? Do you know what his daughter does to me every day?"

"Do you want me to have Manny speak to her?"

I sat up. "No! That will only make things worse. Just do me one favor."

"Anything," Mom said.

"Make sure Angel never finds out her father is dating my mother."

"Manny wants to tell her," Mom said. "He wanted me to tell you, too. Now that you know, I'm sure she'll find out."

I flopped back down onto the bed. "Just leave me here to die then."

"Libby, stop being so dramatic. Everything will be fine."

That was easy for her to say. She didn't have to attend high school with Angel Rivera.

SOMETHING TO BLOG ABOUT

I am still in shock. This is worse than burning my hair in chemistry class. My mother is dating Angel Rivera's father. And I saw Angel's father nearly naked. Sitting in my kitchen. At the same table where I eat every day.

If there is any good fortune in my future, Mr. Rivera will suddenly develop amnesia and forget to tell Angel. Because if she ever finds out, my life is going to be a thousand times worse than it already is. I'll have to move to another continent and change my name. Or at least transfer out of Yeardley High.

"I DON'T UNDERSTAND," KEISHA SAID. WE SAT at a corner table eating a late lunch at Pizza 'N More, which made the best pizza and subs in town. Even though it wasn't very crowded at that time in the afternoon, the music from the old jukebox in the corner was turned up pretty loud. We practically had to yell to hear each other. "Why is it a problem?"

I put down my slice of pepperoni-and-pineapple pizza and looked at her as if she had completely lost her mind. Which, it seemed, she had.

"Because *my* mother is dating *Angel's* father," I explained as if I were talking to a child.

"It's not the greatest situation," Keisha told me, "but it doesn't mean you have to see Angel or anything. Did your mom say she was going to marry this guy?"

"Oh, my God." My pizza landed on my paper plate with a wet smack. "I hadn't even thought about the possibility of *marriage*. Thanks a lot!"

"Sorry," Keisha said, wrapping a string of cheese around her finger. "But as long as they haven't mentioned the M word, you're okay. You don't even have to see Angel outside of school."

"Seeing her dad almost naked was bad enough."

We shuddered at the thought.

"So how is the tutoring going?" Keisha asked.

"It's going great. I'm learning all kinds of things about Seth, like his favorite movie and—"

"I meant how is the *actual* tutoring going?" Keisha said.

"Oh, that. Fine. I think Seth is really starting to catch on to the work."

"And you?"

"I'm understanding things a little better than I did before," I admitted. "*You* should be teaching that class instead of Ms. Hoover."

"Speaking of chemistry," Keisha said through a mouthful of pizza, "I asked everyone in our class if they had seen who put the hearts all over my desk, but no one had any idea. Or they lied if they did. I can't be sure which."

When I reached the starting line again, I bent over gasping. I had pushed myself harder than I usually did during the off-season, and my body burned with the need for air.

"Wow," I heard Seth say as I tried to catch my breath. "How many medals have you won?"

I looked up, pressing a hand into my side to ease the ache. "Medals? Me? None. I'm not that good. Dana Hollingsworth is the medal winner for the girls at this school, not me."

"You really flew around that track," Seth told me.

"Haven't you ever been to any of our track meets?" I asked, grabbing my water bottle and squirting some into my mouth. "Dana's *way* faster than me."

"Going to track meets would require some shred of school spirit, which I don't have." Seth grinned.

I laughed as I rubbed my towel along my neck. "You don't need school spirit, just the desire to see another school get their butts kicked."

"Now you sound like Keisha." Seth laughed at his own joke. "I'll keep that in mind next track season."

I jogged a few more laps around the track before returning to the bleachers. Seth had his chemistry book open on his lap and was writing in his notebook.

"I don't know who invented chemistry, but he was

obviously insane," Seth commented as I did my cooldown stretches. "What is with all these formulas and chemical compounds? Why can't they just say salt instead of saying N-A-C-L?"

"The real question is, when will we ever need to know the chemical compound for salt after high school?" I asked. "I don't know about you, but I don't plan on being a scientist in the future."

"Same here."

I finished my stretches and toweled off, then drank long gulps of water. When I was done, I sat down on the bleachers, trying not to sit too close to Seth in case I smelled bad after all the running and sweating.

Seth pointed to the periodic table on the page he had open. "Like I'm ever going to figure this thing out," he muttered.

"It's not that bad," I said, taking the book from him. "The thing to remember is that the elements are laid out in order of their atomic weight."

Thank you, Keisha, for a brief overview of the periodic table during lunch on Friday.

"And some of the elements are easy to remember," I went on. "Like H-E for helium and N-I for nickel. But others are tricky. Take gold, for example. Its letters are A-U, which makes no sense, but supposedly it has something to do with Latin. We just have to memorize the tricky ones."

Seth sighed. "Like we don't have plenty of things to do other than try to remember all of this stuff so we can pass the tenth grade."

"And so we can stay on the track team," I said. "I have to keep my grades up or else I won't be able to run, no matter how fast I am."

Seth made a face. "I told you I have no school spirit. I'd rather fail chemistry than try to figure all of this out just to compete on a school sports team."

I laughed. "Okay, then, what *do* you do during the time you're avoiding school athletic events?"

"Nothing much," Seth said, shrugging. "I help my dad out with his work sometimes. He's a mechanic and he also does some odd jobs on the side on the weekends. *And* I play chauffer for my grandma so she can visit all her friends."

I couldn't help laughing. "You drive your *grandmother* around town?"

"She's a pretty cool old lady." Seth grinned. "She's still best friends with a woman she's known since the first grade. I pick them up and take them down to the senior center to dance with all the eligible bachelors every Friday afternoon. And then I get suckered into dancing, too. It started when I was a kid. My grandma would pick me up and take me down there so she could show me off to all of her friends. But now that I have my driver's license, I pick her up instead."

I tried to imagine the cool, flirty Seth dancing with his little grandmother, but it was just too adorable. How could he really be this cute?

Seth glanced at his watch and then took the chemistry book back from me. "I should get going . . . Hey, what are you doing this afternoon?"

My heart pounded against my ribs as if I had run another lap around the track. "Nothing," I said, trying to sound casual. "Why?"

"I'm going to see that new comedy at the mall cinema at three," Seth said. "You should come. You know, if you're not doing anything."

Was Seth asking me out? Was this a date or—

"A bunch of people from school will be there," he continued, shrugging. "Angel talked me into going. Says she'll pay for my ticket and popcorn."

The idea of sitting in the theater, watching Angel try to put her hands all over Seth, did *not* sound like a great time.

"Oh," I said, willing my voice to stay neutral. "I don't think I can make it."

Seth nodded as he stood. "That's okay. I don't know

how good the movie is going to be anyway. I'll see you at school on Monday."

I watched Seth walk across the lawn, forcing myself not to start crying. Seth wasn't interested in me. He had Angel and her disciples following him around. Even if he thought they were annoying, he could always shut them up with kisses. It wasn't like Angel and her friends weren't twenty times hotter than I'd ever be—especially when I was sweaty and smelly, like I was at that moment.

I suddenly felt the need to run another lap. I had to do something to get the image of Seth and Angel out of my head.

SOMETHING TO BLOG ABOUT

I barely made it through my classes this morning. I'm too excited to eat lunch and I'm pretty sure I failed the pop quiz in history.

But I don't care because I'M GOING HOME WITH SETH THIS AFTERNOON!!!

He asked me at the beginning of chemistry. "Hey, Libby, I have to go home right after school today. Do you mind if we study at my house this afternoon instead?"

Do I mind? This is only the most exciting thing that's ever happened to me!

I will never, no matter if I live to be four hundred and two years old, forget the look on Angel's face when Seth invited me to go to his house. It was worth every nasty thing she's ever said or done to me.

104

SETH WAS WAITING ON THE LOW WALL
that separated the paved parking lot from the field when I
walked out of school that afternoon.

"Hey," he said as he zipped his brown corduroy jacket all
the way up, the ends of his hair curling around his collar.

"Thanks for agreeing to come over," Seth said as we
walked across the parking lot. "I thought about just canceling
this afternoon, but I really need the tutoring."

I tried to focus on what he was saying, but it was hard
because I was aware that several girls were watching us leave
together. They all gave me the same look—disbelief mixed
with jealousy. I knew they were all thinking the same thing:
How had a nobody like me gotten the attention of Seth
Jacobs? While everyone seemed to think he was a nice guy

and a great catch, he was still a bit of a mystery. No one knew much about his personal life.

It was just a tutoring session, but the ogling girls didn't know that. They watched us walk side by side toward Seth's beat-up, faded blue Jeep, covered with a layer of dirt. It sounded terrible when he started it up—I loved it immediately.

"So," I said once we were on our way to his house, "you have something you have to do at home this afternoon?"

"I have to watch my sister," he told me. "She usually has dance classes after school, but her dance teacher called this morning to cancel today. My dad and stepmom both work, so I have to play babysitter."

I had certainly never imagined Seth taking care of his little sister.

"How old is she?" I tried to make conversation, asking anything that popped into my head. I clasped my hands between my knees so he wouldn't see them shaking.

"Seven," he told me. "Her name is Jessica. She's my half-sister, my dad and stepmom's daughter."

"Do you live with your dad?" I asked.

Seth nodded slightly. "Yeah. My mom took off when I was really young."

"Oh. I'm sorry."

"It's okay," Seth said, shrugging. "I don't remember much about her."

"My dad left, too," I told him. "Before I was born. I've never met him."

Seth glanced over at me as he pulled to a stop at a red light. "Really?"

I nodded. "Yeah. My mom met him while she was in college. You know, one thing led to another and my mom ended up pregnant and my dad couldn't get away fast enough. I've never even seen a picture of him."

"My mom decided she didn't like being married," Seth said after a long moment of silence. He stared straight ahead, his knuckles turning white as he gripped the steering wheel. "Or being a mother. That's actually how I started dancing with my grandma at the senior center. She began taking me with her after my mom left. I guess to make me forget for a little while." He let out an uncomfortable laugh. "You know, I've never told anyone from school about that before now."

I decided to change the subject because of Seth's strained tone. "Do you get along with your stepmother?" I thought about the possibility of my mom getting married someday and dealing with a stepfather. I'd never had a father in my life, so I didn't know if I wanted one.

"As good as can be expected. I don't resent her for marrying my dad or anything like that. She's nice and she treats me the same as she does Jessica, so I guess I can't complain too much."

"Here we are," Seth said after a few minutes. He turned the Jeep into the driveway of a modest ranch-style home with a wooden swing on the front porch.

Seth led me inside. I stood for a moment in the entryway, taking a good look at the home I'd stepped into. Seth's house looked surprisingly normal. A blue couch with a small tear on one armrest sat along the wall. A recliner was turned to face a large TV. Magazines lay scattered across the coffee table. Toys spilled from a box in the corner.

I noticed a family portrait on the wall near the door. A man and woman were seated in the center of the photo, with Seth standing in the background and a little blond girl standing in the front.

"Is this your family?" I asked.

Seth nodded. "Yeah. You want something to drink before we start?"

I nodded. "Okay. Whatever you have is fine."

While Seth disappeared into the kitchen, I wondered what to do. Should I go ahead and sit on the couch, prop my feet up, and act as though I were at my own home?

I surveyed the living room. If I sat in the recliner, there was no way Seth could sit near me, so there'd be no chance for kissing.

The thought of kissing Seth sent a shiver of nervousness and excitement down my spine.

Okay, Libby, focus, I told myself. This is a tutoring session, so we'll need to sit near each other anyway. Just sit on the couch.

Seth came back into the room, carrying two cans of Coke.

We opened our chemistry books and started reading the next chapter. We were all the way up to chapter three, and I had to admit that even *I* was beginning to understand this foreign language called chemistry. I might even do well on the midterm that was less than three weeks away, as Ms. Hoover kept reminding us.

We hadn't been studying long before the front door swung open and the little girl from the family portrait skipped into the room. She stopped when she saw me, her blond ponytail swinging around to hit her cheek.

"Ooooh!" she squealed, grinning wide. She had the same smile as her older brother. "Seth has a girlfriend!"

"Jess, I told you about Libby already," Seth said. The tips of his ears looked a little pink. "She's tutoring me in chemistry. You remember what tutoring means, right?"

"It means you like to kiss her!" Jessica shrieked. She skipped down the hall, making loud kissing noises.

I knew I was blushing. And I could barely contain myself over the fact that Seth had told her about me. "She's cute," I said calmly.

Seth ducked his head and adjusted the chemistry book in his lap. "Sorry about that. She can be a pest sometimes, but she's usually okay."

"I understand," I told him. "My cousin Roger has a younger brother and sister, so I know how little kids can be."

We tried to get back to studying, but after only a few minutes of peace and quiet, we heard kissing noises again. Jessica had snuck into the living room and was hiding behind the recliner, peeking out at us.

Seth pulled her to her feet. "How about you eat a snack in the kitchen and leave us alone for a little while?" he asked as he dragged his sister out of the room.

Jessica did leave us alone long enough to work through most of the chapter. But finally, she couldn't stand it any longer and wanted some attention. She showed me the dance she was learning for a recital and took me to her room to show me all her stuffed animals. I peeked into Seth's room as we passed, but all I saw was an unmade bed, with clothes and books scattered all over the floor.

After the tour of Jessica's room, Seth decided it was time to take me home.

"Shotgun!" Jessica yelled as she raced out to the Jeep.

"No, Jess, Libby gets to sit in the front," Seth told her.

Jessica crossed her arms over her chest and stomped her feet. "I said shotgun!"

"You can ride shotgun on the way back," he told her.

Jessica stuck out her lower lip, but she climbed into the back and buckled her seat belt. She chattered nonstop about her recital on the way to my apartment. When we pulled into the parking lot in front of my building, Jessica wanted to go up to see my room, but Seth said no.

He looked over at me and smiled.

I grinned back like an idiot.

After a moment, Seth said, "See you at school."

I remembered we were in front of my apartment. "Oh!

Right." I fumbled with the door handle before I finally got it open and climbed out of the car. "See you tomorrow."

"Bye!" Jessica called as she tumbled over the console while trying to get into the front seat. She pressed her face against the window, blowing on the glass to make her cheeks puff out as Seth pulled away.

SOMETHING TO BLOG ABOUT

I should have smelled a trap.

My mother brought home a pizza covered with pepperoni and pineapple. I smelled it as soon as she walked into the apartment carrying the pizza box and a bag containing a movie I really wanted to see.

But I guess I was still so distracted about going to Seth's house yesterday that I wasn't really thinking. I mean, all day I've been replaying every word he said to me—the things he told me about his mom walking out on him and his dad, and his spending time with his grandmother at the senior center, and just thinking about the sound of his voice while we studied.

So it was totally unfair of Mom to ambush me when my mind was preoccupied with such precious thoughts.

I TOOK TWO SLICES OF PIZZA AND A COKE, and settled on the couch while Mom put the DVD in.

We were only twenty minutes into the movie when Mom said, "Libby, I have a favor to ask you."

I was feeding Homer some cheese from my pizza. He swatted at the string hanging from my finger before biting it. "Huh?" I asked.

"Manny wants to have dinner at his house this weekend," she said. "Saturday."

"That sounds nice," I said. "Is he going to set out candles and buy you roses?"

"No," Mom said. "Not a *romantic* dinner. A family dinner. You and me, and him and Angel."

I had just taken a sip of Coke and started to cough, spraying soda everywhere. Mom slapped my back.

"*What?*" I asked when I could talk again.

"He wants the four of us to have dinner together . . . So we can all meet and get to know each other."

Had my mother lost her mind? Did she not see she was stepping into dangerous territory?

"I know more than I want to about Angel," I told her. Homer finished his cheese and chomped down on my finger.

"Libby," Mom said. "I think it would be nice for all of us to spend some time together. Manny would like to get to know you, and I'd like to meet Angel."

"No, Mom. Stay far, far away from Angel." Going along with Angel's plans to break our parents up was one thing. No way could I let my mom be exposed to her in person.

"I know," I said, "Manny can come over here and we'll cook for him. Just me, you, and him. No Angel."

Mom gave me a look. "Angel is Manny's daughter. We can't leave her out."

"I think she'd prefer to be left out," I muttered.

"What?"

"Nothing." I grabbed my mom's hands even though my fingers were greasy. "Mom, *please* don't make me do this. I can't spend my Saturday night with Angel Rivera! Do you know what she did to me today? She stuck toilet paper into the waistband of my jeans without my noticing. So I walked around with *toilet paper* hanging from my butt for ten minutes before Keisha pulled it off. Do you really want to meet someone like that?"

"If she does things like that, there has to be a reason for it," Mom told me. "Maybe she's jealous of you."

"The reason is she's psycho!" I exclaimed.

"I don't want to hear any more of this from you," Mom said, her brow wrinkled. "We are going to the Riveras' Saturday night. No complaints. No bad-mouthing Angel. Got it?"

I slumped into the couch and stared at the TV. "Got it," I mumbled.

SOMETHING TO BLOG ABOUT

I KNEW I should never have gotten involved in Angel's plans. I KNEW she was evil. Why did I let myself get mixed up in this? I'm claiming temporary insanity. Our parents' dating has messed up my brain and caused me to do stupid things, like thinking that any plan of Angel's could lead to anything good.

NOW SHE'S GOTTEN ME SUSPENDED FROM SCHOOL AND GROUNDED!

I absolutely despise Angel Rivera more than anyone else on this earth.

117

ROGER FOUND ME AS I CROSSED THE FRONT lawn of Yeardley High on Thursday morning. "Hey," he said. "Did Keisha say anything about the Raisinettes I left for her?"

I had IM'd with Keisha the night before and she had gone on and on about this basket of Raisinettes that were left on her front porch.

"She told me she found them when she got home," I said. "Why don't you ever give me Raisinettes? You know I like them, too. *And* I'm your favorite cousin."

"Hmm, seeing as how you're my *only* cousin, I guess you are," Roger told me. "Keisha didn't say anything? Like how her mom saw me dropping the Raisinettes off?"

"No, Keisha said her mom didn't hear anyone come into the yard."

Roger let out a deep breath. "Good. I had almost gotten away, but then Mrs. Jones opened the front door and saw me. I had to tell her what I was doing." He cringed. "Do you know how embarrassing it is to tell a girl's mother that you're playing secret admirer?"

"Well, apparently Mrs. Jones didn't say anything to Keisha," I told him.

"She said she wouldn't, but I was a little worried that she might let it slip out. She thought the whole thing was 'adorable.' Her word, not mine."

"It *is* kind of ador—"

I was interrupted when Angel appeared in my path. I could see the fury in her eyes. "I need to talk to you," she told me. *"Now."*

"What about?" Roger asked.

Angel didn't even look at him. "This is between Elizabeth and me." She grabbed my arm and pulled me away.

Roger started after us, but I shook my head at him. "I'll see you later," I called.

Angel didn't stop until we had rounded the corner of

the main building, away from the groups of kids milling on the front lawn. She pushed me against the brick wall.

"Have fun the other day?"

"Doing what?"

"Don't play innocent with me. I saw you going to Seth's house."

I shrugged. "I'm tutoring him in chemistry."

"Oh, I don't doubt that there was chemistry of some sort involved," Angel said. She leaned toward me, her lips set in a straight line. "Look, everyone knows Seth is all flirting and no action. If anyone is ever going to snag him, it'll be me, his best friend for the last six years. So don't think someone like you has any chance with him."

My heart thumped a mile a minute, but I tried not to let it show as I looked up at her and took a deep breath. "Maybe you should mind your own business, Angel. Whatever does or doesn't happen between Seth and me is no concern of yours."

I started to walk away, but Angel grabbed my arm. "I'm not done with you yet. What is this about dinner on Saturday?"

"Don't remind me," I told her. "My mom sprang that surprise on me last night."

"How did they even arrange that? You *are* intercepting the calls, aren't you?"

"Yes," I told her, "but your dad hasn't called recently. Maybe they're talking to each other during the day."

Angel's face contorted into an ugly scowl as she paced the grass in front of me.

"This dinner absolutely *cannot* happen. You got me? It's one thing for them to see each other on their own, but it's entirely different for them to get us involved."

I watched her pace. "Why is that different?"

Angel stopped and spun around to face me again. "Because once they get us involved, that means it's serious between them. That means they might even start discussing the possibility of all of us being involved *permanently*."

I guess she could see that I still wasn't catching on, because she exclaimed, "They might get married, you idiot!"

"I'm not an idiot!" I snapped. "And there is no way I will ever allow my mother to marry a Rivera."

"Well, that's perfect because there's no way I'd ever let my father legally attach himself to such trash."

My hands were balled into fists at my sides. "Don't talk about my mother like that," I said through clenched teeth.

Angel smirked at me. "That's good. Hold on to that anger. Because now it's time for phase two. I'll see you this afternoon."

With that, she disappeared around the side of the building.

As I headed toward my sixth-period class, I heard someone call my name. When I stopped and looked back, Angel stormed up to me with a strange look in her eyes.

"What do you want?" I asked.

"Keep your loser mother away from my father!" Angel shouted, glaring down at me. Several people stopped at her outburst and looked at us.

I shifted my books from one arm to the other. "I told you this morning not to call my mom names."

Angel reached out and pushed me so hard that I stumbled backward. I would have fallen if it weren't for a group of football players standing behind me, who helped me regain my balance.

"What is your problem?" I asked Angel.

"My problem is that no one named Fawcett will ever marry my father. Not as long as I have something to say about it."

I rolled my eyes at her and started to turn away.

"Whatever. I'm going to class, Angel."

But I never made it more than two steps. The full weight of Angel's tall body landed on my back, sending the both of us tumbling to the floor. I twisted around to find Angel straddled on top of me. She grabbed fistfuls of my hair and pulled, shook my head, and screamed at me. I had never been involved in a fight before, but I'd seen plenty in the halls of Yeardley High. And if I had the choice between fighting a guy or fighting a girl, I'd pick the guy any day. Girls fought dirty—pulling hair and scratching skin. And that was exactly what Angel did. She was like a rabid animal.

I tried to shield my face, uncertain whether I should fight back or not.

"Ow!" I shrieked as Angel tugged hard at my hair. I reached up and managed to grab some of hers to pull back.

I don't know how, but I ended up on top of Angel. I should have stood up and ended it, but I didn't. Adrenaline pumped through my body and I was shaking and crying and screaming at her as I scratched my short nails down her arms.

The crowd gathered around to cheer us on, yelling and shrieking like guys do whenever girls fight. I barely heard them as Angel and I twisted together on the floor.

Suddenly, I was pulled off of Angel and into the air, kicking. Mr. Evans, the art teacher, snatched Angel to her feet. Coach Rouse, the football coach, took hold of me.

"Get to class!" Coach Rouse bellowed at the crowd. The students split up faster than I had ever seen them move outside of a track meet.

Neither Coach Rouse nor Mr. Evans said anything to Angel or me as they dragged us down the hall and to the principal's office. We sat in hard chairs for a long time while Mr. Evans and Coach Rouse talked to the principal, Mr. Davenport. Angel acted as if this had been no big deal. Her hair was a rat's nest on one side and she had a scratch down her otherwise flawless right cheek, but she just sat there, with her usual smirk, and that's when I realized that *this* was her plan. This was phase two, the part I'd had a bad feeling about. And now I understood why Angel never warned me about it. If I had known she intended for us to fight in school, I would never have gone along with it.

Usually, if you got into minor problems at school, you saw Ms. Wilkins, the assistant principal. But if you were in *huge* trouble, you had to face Mr. Davenport.

So I knew this was major when we were escorted to his office.

Mr. Davenport looked down at two folders on his desk.

I could see my name on one and Angel's on the other. We sat in silence in front of him, in these stuffed leather chairs that I was sure the school board had spent more on than they did our textbooks.

The seconds clicked by. I snuck a glance at Angel from the corner of my eye. She sat smirking, still not bothering to fix her hair.

This was how Mr. Davenport terrorized kids. He let them sit silently in his office until they couldn't handle it any longer and burst out with confessions.

Just when I was ready to confess to stealing a paper clip from my English teacher, Mr. Davenport looked up from the folders and cleared his throat.

"Miss Fawcett, Miss Rivera," he said slowly in his deep voice. "I'm quite surprised at what happened in the east hall."

He looked at us as if waiting for a response. I squirmed in my chair.

"Miss Rivera," he said, looking down at the papers again, "it seems you have been to Ms. Wilkins's office a few times in the past. Never for fighting, mostly just public displays of affection, which, I remind you, are prohibited in school."

I choked back a laugh.

"And Miss Fawcett, you have never caused a problem

before. Your teachers have always written notes about what a pleasure you are to have in their classes."

He folded his hands together on his desk and looked at us over the top of his glasses. "So why, then, are the two of you in my office today?"

I waited for Angel to confess how she'd jumped me in the hall, but she didn't utter a sound. How could she remain so cool and collected under Mr. Davenport's glare?

"Coach Rouse told me that he found you hitting Angelina," Mr. Davenport said.

No way was I going down for this.

"She started it," I said, pointing toward Angel. "I was minding my own business, trying to get to class, when she jumped on top of me and started pulling my hair."

"Crybaby," Angel muttered.

I had an overwhelming urge to leap on top of her again, so I gripped the arms of my chair.

"Angelina?" Mr. Davenport asked. "Is that true?"

Angel didn't say anything.

Mr. Davenport pursed his lips and nodded. "All right then. We'll wait until your parents arrive."

Our parents!

"Mr. Davenport," I said, "*please* don't call my mom. I'll

do anything. I'll—I'll clean the entire school myself. Please, can't we resolve this without our parents?"

"I'm sorry, Elizabeth. Your parents are already on their way."

I slumped back in my chair. "My name is Libby," I muttered.

Our parents arrived at the same time. Mr. Davenport's secretary announced them just before they burst through the office door. Had they been together when they got the call?

Mom rushed to me while Mr. Rivera went over to Angel.

"Are you all right?" Mom asked, checking me over for injuries. My scalp hurt where Angel had pulled my hair and I had a few light scratches, but other than that I was fine.

Mr. Davenport cleared his throat. "Mr. Rivera, Mrs. Fawcett—"

"Ms. Fawcett," Mom corrected him.

"Elizabeth and Angelina were caught fighting in the hall between classes," Mr. Davenport finished. "It was witnessed by at least two dozen students, as well as two members of the faculty."

Mom looked at me. "Libby, what happened? What did you do?"

What did *I* do?

"You think this was my fault?" I exclaimed. "*She* attacked *me*!"

"Settle down," Mom told me. She looked between Angel and me, then turned back to Mr. Davenport. "What are you going to do about this?"

Mr. Davenport looked grim. "The punishment for the first incident of fighting is a one-day suspension."

I stared at him, my mouth hanging open. I had never been faced with the possibility of suspension in my life. This couldn't be happening to me. It was all Angel's fault.

"Both Elizabeth and Angelina will be given one day's suspension," Mr. Davenport said. "I will release them into your care now, if you'd like."

"Thank you," Mr. Rivera said. He stood behind Angel, one hand resting on her shoulder. "I'm sorry for this. I think it may have been caused by a personal situation outside of school."

"We're . . . involved," Mom said as she gestured toward Mr. Rivera. "Manny—I mean, Mr. Rivera and I. We've been dating. For the last few months."

"I don't think he needs to know the details," Mr. Rivera said, trying to keep a smile on his face.

"I only thought it might help," Mom said. "If the girls are fighting at school, their principal deserves to know why."

"I don't think it's necessary to get the school involved in our personal lives," Mr. Rivera said through clenched teeth.

As I gazed at our parents, I realized the brilliance of Angel's plan. Our fighting had caused a problem between them. They were forced to take sides.

Angel caught me looking at her. She smiled and nodded slightly.

She could be a genius sometimes.

"Let's go, Dad," Angel said, directing a black scowl toward me. "I can't stand to be near such filth any longer."

"I guess you should find a way to separate yourself from your body then," I said.

A muscle twitched in Mr. Rivera's jaw. "Let's go," he said, nodding good-bye to Mr. Davenport.

When we got home, Mom exploded.

"Elizabeth Aiden Fawcett!" she shouted. Homer had been sitting in the doorway of the living room, but he bolted away at Mom's voice. "Fighting? I don't remember raising my daughter to fight in school!"

"It wasn't my fault!" I protested. "I tried to walk away, but Angel jumped on me!"

"And you fought back! I don't think Angel scratched her own face!"

"What was I supposed to do, let her hit me without defending myself?"

Mom sucked in a deep breath and then let it out slowly. Her face was crimson and she shook slightly. I'd never seen her this angry.

"You are suspended for one day," Mom said in a lower voice. "And you're grounded for a week."

"That's not fair!" Mom walked into the kitchen and I stomped after her. "This is not my fault!"

"You participated." Mom opened a cabinet and pulled down a bag of Oreo cookies. "Now I suggest you get out of my sight unless you want to make it two weeks."

I stomped to my room and slammed the door.

Well, at least now there was no way Mom could make me go to the Riveras' for dinner on Saturday.

SOMETHING TO BLOG ABOUT

Keisha and Roger both called, but Mom wouldn't let me talk to them. She said I was grounded and couldn't use the phone. So I was surprised when she knocked on my door a few minutes ago to tell me I had a phone call.

"It's Seth Jacobs," Mom said when I opened the door. "He says he needs to talk about your tutoring sessions. But you are only to talk about school, got it?"

I nodded and hurried to the phone. Whatever. I'll agree to anything as long as I have the chance to talk to Seth.

Mom stood nearby, not even trying to hide the fact that she was listening.

Seth knew about the fight. Word had certainly spread fast.

He wanted to know if we were still on for tutoring, so I covered the receiver with my

SOMETHING TO BLOG ABOUT

hand and asked Mom if I was still allowed to tutor Seth next week.

"Is there actual tutoring involved?" Mom asked. "Or is it just a make-out session?"

If I weren't already in trouble, I would have made a face at her smug expression.

Mom gave me permission to tutor Seth, but for one hour only, and I was to come straight home after.

Before we hung up, Seth asked how bad I maimed Angel. I told him she had a pretty big scratch on her face. Thankfully, he said she probably deserved it, since he knows she can be bratty at times.

At least someone is on my side!

- ABOUT
- RECENT POSTS
- SEPTEMBER
- OCTOBER

MY RIBS REALLY HURT

KEEPING SECRETS IS HARD WORK

MYSTERY MAN

MY MOM DID MY LAUNDRY!

KILL ME NOW

AFTERMATH

COUNTDOWN TO MY DOOM

WORST DAUGHTER EVER

FLOWERS STRESS ME OUT

SECOND THOUGHTS

BEST DAY EVER!

AMBUSHED

ANGEL RIVERA IS PURE EVIL

MY ONE PHONE CALL

SOMETHING TO BLOG ABOUT

FRIDAY, OCTOBER 19, 5:20 PM
MY MOM IS SO LAME

After Mom left for work this morning, I looked at the list she'd given me.

- Wash and fold laundry.
- Empty dishwasher and load in breakfast dishes.
- Sweep, mop, and vacuum floors.
- Change bedding on both beds.
- Clean litter box.
- Start dinner at 4:30.

I thought Mom would have been more creative than that, like making me scrub every speck of dirt out of the house with my toothbrush or clean the humongous collection of porcelain frogs in her room. But no. My mom doesn't even know how to dish out punishment correctly.

133

MOM WALKED THROUGH EACH ROOM OF THE apartment when she got home from work, making sure everything was as it should be. She even checked to see if the TV was still on the channel she had left it. (It was.)

"Well," Mom said after she had finished her inspection, "thank you for sticking to your punishment, Libby."

"No problem," I said, smiling brightly. Surprisingly, I was in a good mood. I hadn't gotten into trouble for watching TV or using my computer and it was finally the weekend. A weekend free of Angel. Being suspended wasn't so bad.

We sat down to eat. Mom didn't mention the fight and I certainly wasn't about to bring it up.

While I was clearing away our dishes, I heard the doorbell chime. Mom went to answer it.

"Hello, Ms. Fawcett," I heard Keisha's voice. "I brought Libby her schoolwork from today."

"Thank you, Keisha," Mom said. "Come in. You can talk to Libby for a few minutes, but then I'll have to ask you to leave."

Keisha walked into the kitchen carrying a stack of textbooks and papers. She dropped them on the counter. "I went around to your classes and got your assignments."

"Thanks," I said, making a face at the books. "Hey, Mom, is it all right if we go to my room and talk?"

"Five minutes," Mom answered.

I carried the books to my room with Keisha at my heels.

"So does everyone know about the fight?" I asked.

Keisha nodded. "It was all over school before the end of the day yesterday. What happened anyway? People are saying you drop-kicked Angel."

"I wish I had," I said. "Angel created this plan to get our parents to break up, but she didn't warn me that she was going to jump me in the hall. I'm an innocent victim in this."

"You guys are really trying to break your parents up?" Keisha asked, blinking at me.

I shrugged. "What would you do if your mom was dating Angel's dad?"

"I don't know. I guess I'd want my mother to be happy. Would it matter what I thought?"

Keisha's parents had been married twenty years, so she had no idea what it was like to face the possibility of stepparents—or worse, a stepsister like Angel.

"She's my mother," I said. "She should want *me* to be happy."

"But doesn't she deserve happiness, too?"

I picked at a piece of lint on my bedspread, unable to meet Keisha's gaze. "It doesn't matter anyway. Mom and Mr. Rivera didn't seem very happy yesterday when they came to pick us up. And they didn't talk on the phone last night. I think this problem may be over."

There was a knock on the door and Mom stuck her head in. "Time's up," she said.

Keisha nodded and stood up. "See you Monday, Libby. Bye, Ms. Fawcett."

I stared at the door for a while after she left. I had been pleased that Mom's relationship might be over, but now Keisha's words had made me feel terrible. My mom *did* deserve happiness. Was it right for me to take that away from her, even if I hated Angel?

SOMETHING TO BLOG ABOUT

Mom was already up when my alarm clock went off this morning. She sat at the kitchen table drinking coffee and looked up at me when I entered the room. I was dressed in my usual running outfit: a sweatshirt and yoga pants and sneakers.

This was how our conversation went:

Mom: Where do you think you're going?

Me: Running. Like I do every Saturday.

Mom: Not this Saturday. You're grounded, remember?

Me: I can't go running?

Mom: You can run inside the apartment.

But I can't do that because of Mr. Wetherby, our downstairs neighbor. He bangs on the ceiling with the end of a broomstick

SOMETHING TO BLOG ABOUT

whenever he thinks we're making too much noise. My running in the apartment would probably give him a stroke.

Mom wouldn't even let me run in the parking lot. So I turned around and announced I was going back to bed.

Mom: Be ready at five.

Me: Ready for what?

Mom: Dinner with Manny and Angel. Remember?

Me: We're still going over there? After what happened two days ago? But I'm grounded! I can't leave the apartment!

Mom: You can leave with my supervision. And we're going to the Riveras' at five. So be ready.

Just when I thought things couldn't get any worse! How could my mom not see that there was no way Angel and I could sit through dinner together. (Any sane person could see

138

SOMETHING TO BLOG ABOUT

that.) But no, my mother thought it would be good for us to spend quality time together! Why, so Angel could rip out another handful of my hair? As if my head hasn't been traumatized enough lately.

SOMETHING TO BLOG ABOUT

I have to admit, I am a bit curious about what Angel's house looks like. What does the room of a monster look like? There must be something there that makes her evil because her dad doesn't seem that bad. I mean, maybe Mr. Rivera's not Father of the Year or anything, but at least he's never walked out on her. My dad just didn't care. I have no idea what he even looks like or where he lives. Seth's mom didn't care, either. She totally abandoned him. I think that's part of the reason he keeps to himself sometimes. At least Angel has things slightly better than we do. She doesn't have to deal with the knowledge that one of her parents never wanted her. If anyone has the right to be nasty and start fights in the halls, it should be me. Or Seth.

AT FOUR FORTY-FIVE P.M., MOM FOUND ME lying facedown on my bed. I was dressed in jeans and my favorite *Star Wars* shirt, my shoes on my feet but the laces not tied.

"Why aren't you ready yet?" Mom asked.

I lifted my head from the cocoon of pillows and said, "I am."

Mom lifted one eyebrow. "Excuse me, but I don't call that a proper 'I'm having dinner with my mother's boyfriend for the first time' outfit."

"That's because I call it my 'I'm ready to face my own death' outfit. Queen Amidala gives me the courage to face anything, as long as there's a cute guy at the end of the road. I have a cute guy waiting for me on Monday afternoon, so I guess that counts. Hopefully he won't turn into Darth Vader."

Mom clearly did not find this amusing. She crossed her arms over her chest and said, "Get. Dressed. Now."

We left the house after I'd changed into a striped sweater and denim skirt. It seemed to meet Mom's standards. But she went all out: She wore the one really nice black dress she owned. She fastened pearls to her ears and also wore the pearl bracelet that once belonged to her grandmother.

"Not trying too hard, are you?" I asked as we got into the car.

Mom ignored my comment. "I want you to behave tonight, Libby," she said. "No snide comments. No fighting."

"How many times do I have to tell you that she started it?"

"Whatever," Mom said. "Just behave."

"I'm not three years old."

"With all that whining, you could have fooled me."

I sat in silence for the rest of the ride to the Riveras' house.

Fifteen minutes later, Mom pulled the car into the driveway of a big house. Not quite a mansion, but bigger than the houses that my friends lived in. Why would two people need that much space? Mom and I got along fine in our place, and you could fit at least five of our apartment inside that house.

"Remember what I said," Mom whispered to me as we walked to the front porch.

She rang the doorbell. I expected a uniformed butler to open the door, but Mr. Rivera appeared, smiling wide when he saw us.

"Hi!" He hugged Mom and kissed her. I had to look away in case Mr. Rivera decided to stick his tongue down my mom's throat. I didn't know if he would do that right in front of me, but I didn't want to take any chances. Seeing them half-naked together was enough trauma in my life.

"Hello, Libby," Mr. Rivera said. He moved toward me as if he was going to hug me and I automatically took a step back. I know it was rude, but who could blame me for getting out of the way when a Rivera lunged at me? Mr. Rivera paused, then stuck out his hand instead.

"Hello," I said as I shook his hand. I remembered what Mom said about being on my best behavior. "Thank you for inviting us to your *lovely* home. I'm sure dinner will be *magnificent.*"

Mr. Rivera glanced at Mom, his smile frozen on his face. "Oh, um, yes. You're very welcome, Libby. Please do come in."

The devil's lair looked a lot nicer than I imagined it. I didn't see any roaring fires, but I did see a lot of leather furniture and Turkish rugs. The decor was very dark, with deep brown woods and black upholstery.

"Please have a seat," Mr. Rivera said, gesturing toward the leather couch. "I'll go find Angel and she can entertain you while I finish dinner."

"Do you need help?" Mom asked. "In the kitchen?"

Mr. Rivera waved his hand at her. "No, just sit and relax. It'll be done soon."

He left us in the living room alone, so I looked around to take in more of my surroundings. The artwork on the walls was okay. Mostly forest scenes painted with rich colors. I thought one of Angel's paintings would actually look nice in there.

"It smells weird," I said.

"Libby, don't you dare say another word," Mom told me.

Well, it *did* smell weird in there.

Angel shuffled into the room, dressed in jeans and a T-shirt. Why did she get to dress comfortably while I had to look like I was going to church?

Mom stood up, smoothed the wrinkles from her skirt, and smiled as she lifted a hand toward Angel for a handshake. "Hi, I'm Maura Fawcett," she said.

Angel ignored Mom and threw herself down into a chair across from us. She stared first at me, then at Mom.

"So you're my father's latest girlfriend," she said, looking Mom over.

Mom's smile faltered a bit, but then she regained her composure and said, "Am I what you expected?"

"Pretty much," Angel said, sneering. "What are you, ten years younger than he is?"

Mom's cheeks reddened. "Eleven," she answered.

I wanted to tell Mom not to give Angel any fuel for her fire, but I didn't think she would have listened to me anyway.

"My dad always likes them young," Angel said. "It wouldn't surprise me if after he gets rid of you, he finds a girlfriend who's still in college."

Mom sat down, clasping her hands in her lap again and smiling. "So, Angel," she said, "what do you like to do for fun?"

"Torment Elizabeth," Angel said.

She actually said that to my mother.

Angel apparently didn't want to answer any more of Mom's questions. She turned to me. "Did you enjoy your day off, Elizabeth?"

"My name is Libby, *Angelina*," I said through clenched teeth.

"Did your mommy make you do chores to punish you for being bad?"

Mom stared down at her hands, her entire face and neck tomato red.

"Did your father arrange for your lobotomy yet, Angelina?" I asked.

Angel rolled her eyes. "Hilarious, Elizabeth."

Mr. Rivera appeared in the doorway. "Dinner is served, ladies," he announced.

He took Mom's arm and led us into the dining room, where a long table had been set with the nicest china I'd ever seen. It was even better than the china my grandmother stored in her cabinets in case the president ever came to dinner.

The food looked and smelled really good. My stomach growled as I looked at the golden roasted chicken and steaming pasta and vegetables. After everyone had been served, Mr. Rivera attempted to start a conversation.

"So, Libby, Angel tells me that the two of you are in chemistry together."

I swallowed a mouthful of chicken. "Uh-huh," I said.

"You two should study together sometime," Mr. Rivera said. "I remember how tough chemistry was. It always seems easier when you have another brain to help you understand things."

Obviously he had amnesia and had forgotten the fight

in the hall on Thursday. Did he seriously think Angel and I would agree to study together?

But Mom kicked me under the table, so I said, "Uh-huh. Maybe."

"Elizabeth wouldn't be any help to me in chemistry," Angel told her father as she cut her asparagus daintily. "Unless I need tips on how to set my hair on fire."

Mom chewed very slowly next to me, as if bracing herself for what my response might be. I stared down at my plate, biting my tongue to keep myself from saying something back.

"Well," Mr. Rivera said, smiling, "we all have our clumsy moments."

"In Elizabeth's case, clumsy *life*," Angel said.

I plastered on a fake smile and said, "Angelina, I would prefer it if you would call me Libby."

Angel fake-smiled back at me. "I prefer Elizabeth."

I could sense that Mom and Mr. Rivera knew this dinner wasn't going as they planned. "Libby," Mr. Rivera said, "your mom tells me that you run track in the spring. She says you're very good."

I shrugged. "I'm not the star of the team or anything."

"She's too modest," Mom told him. "Libby is very talented."

"I'll have to come out to one of your meets when the season starts," Mr. Rivera said, "to cheer you on."

Angel's head whipped around and she glared at her father. It was darker than any look she had ever given me.

"You volunteer to attend someone else's stupid track meet when you can't even attend your own daughter's art show in two weeks?" she shouted.

Mr. Rivera cleared his throat. "Angel, we discussed this already. I have a very important case I'm working on right now."

"Yet you can so easily block out time for her track meet months from now when you don't even know what you'll be doing then?" Angel snapped.

"You have five art shows a year," Mr. Rivera said. A vein had appeared in his forehead and he clenched his fork as if he might stab someone with it. "I'll be at the next one."

"That's what you say every time," Angel muttered.

The table was silent for a moment. Mom wiped her mouth with her napkin and said, "What night is the show, Angel? I'd love to see your work."

Angel gave my mom a look that would have stopped my heart cold. "No thanks. I don't need your pity. You're my father's current fling of the month, so don't get too comfortable in his arms. I've seen plenty of women before you and I'll see plenty more."

Mr. Rivera threw down his napkin and stood. "Angelina, I'd like to see you in the kitchen." The vein in his forehead throbbed, pulsating as if it were about to burst through his skin at any moment.

Angel stood. "Don't bother. I'm going to my room."

Her father started after her, but Mom grabbed his arm. "Maybe you should let her have time to herself," she suggested.

Mr. Rivera sat back down. "I apologize for her behavior."

"It's all right," Mom told him. "I'm sure it isn't easy on her, not having a mother and you being so busy with work."

Angel insulted everyone in the room and all my mother could say was that it wasn't easy on her because she didn't have a mother? If I had done that, Mom would have grounded me until I was forty. What about *me*? Wasn't it hard on me having to see my mortal enemy's father want to stick his tongue down my mom's throat right in front of me? And being tormented at school every day?

Angel didn't come out of her room the rest of the night.

We finished dinner and then Mom and I left. I had thought we might hang around longer so she could spend time with Mr. Rivera, but she seemed eager to go. To tell the truth, Mr. Rivera seemed a little relieved when Mom said it was time for us to leave. I made sure to thank him as we left—I hated to admit that he was pretty nice, and he had cooked a delicious dinner.

I thought for sure that Mom would apologize for blaming me for the fight, now that she had seen the wrath of Angel Rivera. But she didn't say one word about it during our ride home or even after we got back to the apartment. Had she not noticed that Angel was evil? Wasn't she ready to give up this relationship yet?

SOMETHING TO BLOG ABOUT

Yeardley High did not, as I had hoped, spontaneously combust during my absence on Friday. It does seem, however, that I have become some sort of celebrity. When I walked into school this morning, kids I didn't even know called out "Hey, Libby!" and "Welcome back, Libby!" Of course, none of them were the popular kids that Angel hangs out with. They all continued their game of pretending that I do not exist.

I tried to say hi and smile at the people who greeted me as I made my way to my locker, but it's getting to be a little too much. I don't even know the names of half of these people! Yet they're smiling as if I'm their best friend in the world and high-fiving me as they walk by. Now I know how celebrities feel!

151

"WHAT IS THE DEAL WITH ALL THESE people?" I asked as I joined Keisha at her locker just before chemistry.

Keisha looked up from a card she was reading. "What people?"

Just then two girls walked by and said, "Hey, Libby! Good to see you're back!"

I gestured toward the girls' backs as they walked away. "Those people. Suddenly I'm Miss Yeardley High."

"Oh, that," Keisha said. "I told you word had gotten around about the fight."

"You didn't say I was a celebrity," I said.

Keisha shrugged. "A lot of people are happy that you did to Angel what they've always dreamed of doing."

I leaned against the locker as more kids called out to

me. "They *do* realize that Angel started the fight? And that Coach Rouse and Mr. Evans broke it up before a winner could be determined?"

"Doesn't matter. You fought back against Angel. And from what I saw as I walked in this morning, you left her with a nasty scratch down her cheek. All the freaks and geeks of Yeardley High worship you now. The popular brats still hate you, but who cares?" She laughed. "You could just kick all their butts, too."

I looked at the card Keisha still held as she pushed around some books in her locker. "What's that?"

She smiled. "Something else from my secret admirer. Look."

She showed me the card, on which were typed the words:

Why is it that
You occupy my mind
Like the Led Zeppelin song
That leaves me feeling fine.
You fill my every thought
All day and through the night.
To have you in my arms
Would make my world right.

"So your secret admirer is a bad poet now?" I asked.

"Led Zeppelin!" Keisha exclaimed. "This guy knows the way to my heart. I think I can forgive him for the flower disaster now."

Okay, so Roger had won her over. All he had to do was reveal himself and everything would be perfect.

By the time I arrived at class, I had a headache and my cheeks hurt from returning so many friendly greetings. I didn't want to speak to anyone else for the rest of the day, I was so worn out. No wonder celebrities attacked the paparazzi.

Angel seemed to have gotten over her ill mood from Saturday night. She actually smiled at me when I walked in. Of course, I knew something was up right away. When had Angel ever smiled at me simply because she felt the need to be nice?

"It seems you're quite popular all of a sudden," she said as I took my seat. "It also seems that people are under the impression that *you* won our fight."

"Whatever, Angel." I rubbed my temples with my fingertips. "I really don't feel like dealing with you today."

She leaned across the aisle toward me, her black hair falling over her shoulders. "Don't think this is over yet," she hissed. "There is no way I'm letting anything continue between my father and that tramp that you call Mommy."

Why did I let her get to me? I should have ignored her. That was the only way to respond to anything Angel said or did. If you took any action, it only made things worse.

Of course Ms. Hoover happened to walk into the room just as I demanded that Angel apologize for what she'd said about my mom or else I'd do more than scratch her face.

So I got detention. My first day back from being suspended because of Angel, and now I had detention because of her.

Life was *so* not fair.

SOMETHING TO BLOG ABOUT

ANGEL, HOW I LOATHE THEE

I don't think I have ever hated someone as much as I hate Angel. I know, I'm not supposed to *hate* anyone, but Angel makes it so easy. She's made it her mission in life to torment me as much as possible. And somehow, whenever she's around, I end up in trouble.

I could be looking forward to an afternoon with Seth, studying chemistry in the library. But no. Thanks to Angel, I have to spend an hour in detention—which I have NEVER been to in my entire life—and suffer through withdrawal because I can't get my daily Seth fix.

DETENTION WAS FAR WORSE THAN suspension. For an hour I had to sit in Room 107 and do my homework. Then when I was done, I had to stare at the wall in order to avoid staring at Mr. Umber's shiny bald head. There was no TV, no computer, no nothing.

There were a few other people in detention with me, including a bunch of kids who'd gotten caught smoking behind the band room.

I sat at the back of the room near two guys who were trying not to be seen sleeping at their desks. Halfway through detention, one of the guys sat up and poked me in the back.

"Hey," he whispered. "Aren't you that girl who beat up Angel Rivera?"

He had blue hair and wore a bunch of black leather

bracelets on one wrist. He didn't look like someone Angel would hang out with, so I figured I didn't have to worry about him wanting to get revenge. "Yeah," I whispered back.

"I only saw the very end of the fight," the guy told me. "But it was awesome! I heard some cheerleaders talking about you on Friday and they were afraid you'd rip out their hair if they ever got in your way."

Cheerleaders were afraid of little old Libby Fawcett? I enjoyed that bit of news so much, I could have kissed that guy.

I practically cheered when the bell rang, signaling the end of the hour. I grabbed my books and hurried out of the room, only to skid to a halt when I spotted Seth seated on the floor in front of the detention room. He was leaning back against the lockers, with his chemistry book open in his lap.

"I figured since we couldn't actually study together today, I'd sit out here and read while you served your sentence," he said when he saw me.

"You don't need me anymore then, do you?" I asked. "You'll be tutoring yourself soon."

Seth stood, tucking his book under his arm. "No way," he said. "I always look forward to our sessions. You should have seen how miserable I was on Friday."

We walked down the hall together. "You were not," I said.

"I was! Ask your friend Roger. I was crying and wandering around the halls. I kept pestering him with questions about when you were coming back."

Was he flirting with me? I couldn't tell. Maybe he was just being friendly, joking like he would with a buddy.

"I'm glad that you value my tutoring that much," I said, laughing.

"And the fact that you're cute doesn't hurt."

Had I heard him right? Did he say I was cute?

I kind of chuckled, trying to play it off in case I was imagining things. "Yeah, sure."

"I'm really glad you agreed to tutor me," Seth said. "If you hadn't, I might have gotten stuck with someone not as nice to look at."

I squeezed my eyes shut, replaying the words in my head. This was not happening. Seth Jacobs was not telling me I was pretty. It wasn't possible.

"Hi, Seth!"

I opened my eyes and watched Angel saunter toward us, a wide grin spread across her face. She wore a shirtdress that showed off her figure just right, with curves I could only dream about having. I snuck a glance at Seth and saw that he, too, noticed her killer body.

"Hi, Angel," Seth greeted her.

Angel slipped her arm through Seth's. "What are you still doing here? I thought you spent as little time as possible at this place."

"There was something I had to do," Seth told her, shrugging.

Angel sneered in my direction and moved around so that she stood between Seth and me. "Hey, are you coming to my party next week?"

"Maybe."

"It wouldn't be any fun without you there," Angel told him, giggling and leaning into his arm.

Seth laughed. "I have a feeling you know how to have fun, whether I'm there or not."

I looked away, clenching my teeth. I couldn't believe it. He was flirting with Angel right in front of me—after he had just flirted with me! He had said they were only friends. Yeah, but they looked like *best* friends.

"Hey, do you have the notes from English?" Seth asked Angel.

"Why didn't you take notes during class?" Angel asked him, poking a finger into his side.

Seth laughed and reached over to tickle her, making her giggle. "I needed to catch up on my sleep."

I felt sick and it wasn't just from watching Angel revel in

Seth's attention. If this was how he treated his friends, then I was nothing special. I was just another girl he had under his spell. He thought I was cute enough to tutor him and help get his grade up, but other than that, I was nothing.

"Libby?" Seth asked. "You okay? You look like your hair just got too close to a Bunsen burner."

Seth's laughter and Angel's snorting filled my ears as I tried to fight back the tears that were forming in my eyes.

"Do I need to unleash Angel on you to snap you out of it?" he asked, laughing. "Let you body-slam her a few times?"

Now he was definitely making fun of me. I didn't have to stand there and take it while Angel kept giving me her stupid smirks.

161

"I have to go." I turned and stomped down the hall, pushing Miguel Sanchez and his trumpet out of my way. He muttered angrily at me in Spanish as he stumbled backward into a row of lockers.

"Libby!" Seth called after me.

But I didn't stop to hear what he had to say. I picked up my pace and stormed out of the front doors, my hands clenched at my sides.

SOMETHING TO BLOG ABOUT

I am seriously considering not going to the tutoring session tomorrow. It would serve him right anyway to lose his car for leading me on like this for the last couple of weeks.

Although I guess he didn't exactly lead me on. He never tried to kiss me or anything. But he did come to visit me at the track more than once, and he took me to his home and told me all these things about himself. You know, I thought we might at least be friends, if nothing else. Real friends, I mean, not "friends" like he is with other girls.

But it turns out I'm not special to him at all. He could replace me with Angel and never know the difference.

And that is the thing that hurts most of all.

I SAW SOMEONE STANDING AT MY LOCKER as I pushed through the crowd the next morning. His back was turned toward me, but I recognized the brown corduroy jacket.

My first thought was to keep walking and not even stop at my locker. But I needed my chemistry book for my homeroom review session with Keisha. And I needed my geometry book because I wouldn't have time to go back to my locker after homeroom was finished.

"Hey, Libby," Seth greeted me. I pushed past him to my locker. I had to stop, but I didn't have to talk to him.

"Why'd you run away like that yesterday?" Seth asked, standing so close I could breathe in his soap smell. I tried not to inhale too much of it so I wouldn't get light-headed from the delicious scent of him.

I still didn't speak, so Seth reached out and turned my face to his. My skin tingled at his touch.

"Hey," he said, his brow creasing as he frowned. "Are you mad at me?"

"I don't like being teased," I snapped. I had the books I needed, so I slammed my locker shut and stomped away.

"Libby!" Seth called out behind me.

Seth kept appearing near my classes all morning, but I wouldn't look at him.

"Maybe you should talk to him," Keisha suggested after second period. "He looks like he's lost his best friend."

"I'm not his friend. I'm his tutor. We barely even know each other."

Sure, he had taken me to his home and introduced me to his sister. And he had told me about how his mom had left when he was little, and I had told him about my dad. And we talked during our tutoring sessions about all kinds of things—people in school, music and movies we liked, my love and his loathing for various Hollywood actors.

But really, what else did I know about him? Nothing except that he always wore that same corduroy jacket and moved his lips when he read. And his hair fell into his face whenever he bent over his chemistry book. And—

Stop. No. He thought he could flirt and I'd do whatever he wanted. I wasn't anyone special to him. He had probably told all those same things to Angel, too.

When I got to chemistry, Seth was already in his seat in the back of the room. He didn't bother trying to talk to me, but I shot him the meanest look I was capable of so he'd know to keep away.

Unfortunately, Roger ruined my glare by telling me, "Libs, no offense, but you look *really* constipated."

Angel thought that was the funniest thing she'd ever heard and asked Ms. Hoover for a hall pass for me so I could go to the bathroom.

"I appreciate your concern for your classmates, Angel," Ms. Hoover said. "But if Libby needs to use the facilities, she can ask me herself."

I didn't dare look back at Seth to see if he'd been listening.

I hid at the computer bank in the library during lunch to avoid seeing Seth. The foot fetish kid wasn't at his usual computer, number nine. He must have been out sick. Everyone was so used to him sitting there that no one else used number nine; it just sat empty, and shoeless.

I got the feeling that someone was watching me. I looked up to see Seth standing at the library doors, staring directly at me.

He had that look on his face like he wanted to talk. I closed my web browser and grabbed my things as I jumped up from the chair. I started to walk quickly toward another exit, but Ms. Taylor called after me.

"You have to sign yourself out when you're done!" she shrieked in a very nonlibrary voice. She waved the clipboard with the computer sign-in sheets at me.

I had no choice but to walk back to her desk and put my sign-out time next to my name on the list. I tried to write quickly, but Seth still caught up to me before I could get away.

"We need to talk," he said.

"I don't want to."

He gently grabbed my arm and pulled me toward him.

"Clearly I've done something to make you upset. I think I deserve to know what that is."

Well, let's see. How about toying with the fragile emotions of a teenager? How about treating me as if I were just like any other dumb girl at this school when I had started to think that maybe I was different, maybe I could be special?

I thought these things and wanted to scream them at Seth, but I couldn't say them out loud. A lump had formed in my throat and tears stung my eyes. My vision blurred so that everything was a blob of fuzzy colors.

"Let me go," I said as I wrenched my arm free of Seth's grasp. I had to get out of the library before I started sobbing in front of everyone.

"Shh!" Ms. Taylor said. "And no running!"

"Libby!" Seth called as I ran toward the door.

"Library voice!" Ms. Taylor screeched.

"Talk to him before I kick both your butts," Keisha said to me after the last bell. "He chased me down and begged me to make you talk to him. Why do think he would use you just because he needed a tutor? Did it ever occur to you that he really does think you're cute and he might *actually* be interested in you?"

"I've lived fifteen years without having any guys interested in me, except two," I explained. "*Two* in fifteen years. One happened to be a boy in my kindergarten class who liked to play with my hair during story time. The other was Andy Cornwall. And do I have to remind you what happened with Andy Cornwall?"

Andy was my boyfriend for a week in fifth grade. He

was a nice boy, but he kissed me at Keisha's birthday party. That was perfectly fine, until he tried to stick his tongue in my mouth. I was so nervous that I threw up. In his lap.

"That was a long time ago," Keisha said. "And the only reason other guys haven't asked you out is because you're too shy. You never notice when a guy flirts with you, so you don't flirt back." Keisha smacked the back of my head. "Wake up, Libby! Seth likes you!"

"Ow." I rubbed my head. "That really hurt."

"Good," Keisha replied.

"Have other guys been interested in me?" I tried to remember if I had ever picked up on any signals. Over the years there had been a few instances where I thought a guy *might* have smiled at me in a more-than-friends way, but I was never certain, so I never did anything.

Keisha was right. I really was clueless when it came to guys.

But this wasn't just any guy. This was *Seth Jacobs*. In the ninth grade I used to write "Libby Jacobs" in my notebooks and then tear up the pages before anyone could see.

But Seth didn't date anyone. He flirted, yes—flirted a lot with all of the idiotic giggly girls at Yeardley High.

Was I so naive to think he was holding out for something special?

"Go talk to him," Keisha said.

So I went to his tutoring session. He sat at our usual table, reading his chemistry book. He looked up when I put my books down.

"I didn't think you'd come," he said.

I sat down. "Look," I began, "I know I'm just some girl who fantasizes about celebrities and secretly listens to boy bands and who probably likes all the things you hate, but I don't like being made a fool of by other people. I do enough of that on my own."

I didn't look at him, but I could feel his eyes on me.

"Libby," he said. "I would never make fun of you."

"Then don't think you can flirt with me like you do with all the other girls. Have an iota of respect for me—" I paused before adding, "Besides, I couldn't be less interested."

The last part was a lie, but I didn't want him to know how interested I really was. I didn't want him laughing later about how stupid I was for thinking we could ever be together.

Seth was silent for a moment. I could hear the people at the computers typing as they secretly logged into chat rooms when Ms. Taylor wasn't looking.

Finally Seth said, "I'm sorry, Libby."

And then we awkwardly worked on chemistry.

Keisha was wrong. How could I have thought that Seth could ever have been interested in me?

I would not be upset. I knew it from the very beginning. I may have been inexperienced in the ways of love, but I was intelligent enough to know that the guy of my dreams would never like me as anything more than his tutor.

Mom knew something was wrong as soon as she got home. She had brought home dinner from our favorite Chinese place: egg rolls and vegetable lo mein and wonton soup. But I only picked at my egg roll during dinner.

Finally, Mom put down the broccoli she had been about to bite into and said, "*Please* talk to me."

I couldn't hold it in anymore. I started crying right into my lo mein. Mom left her seat to pull me into her arms.

She stroked my hair in silence for a while. When my sobs had subsided some, she asked me again what was wrong.

"Seth," I said. "Yesterday, he said I was cute. But then

Angel appeared and he was all flirty with her and I realized that I'm just like all the other girls who follow him around. I mean nothing to him. Keisha said I was crazy and she convinced me that he might actually be interested in me. So I let myself believe that there was the possibility . . ." I buried my face in Mom's shoulder. "But he doesn't like me as anything more than a tutor!"

Mom sighed. "Teenage boys are complicated. You can never tell if they like you or not. And sometimes, they aren't even sure themselves." She kissed the top of my head. "The right boy is out there for you. And when you find him, he'll see how great you are and he won't be afraid to tell you that."

I sat up and wiped my eyes. "That doesn't make me feel any better. I wanted that boy to be Seth."

"I know." Mom returned to her chair but didn't start eating again yet. "Do you think that maybe he really does like you, but your reaction scared him? Maybe *he's* afraid of rejection."

I thought about how Seth could have any girl in school he wanted. He had to notice how Angel and the other beautiful girls looked at him when he walked by. He had to know how good-looking he was.

"I don't think he's worried about rejection. He's just not

interested." I wiped my nose with my napkin. "I have to accept that and move on."

Mom reached over to touch my face. "He'd have to be crazy not to like you."

"I know you're just saying that because you're my mom and you have to."

Mom shook her head. "You don't know how amazing you are."

"Amazing enough to be released from house arrest?" I asked.

"Not that amazing," Mom told me, taking a bite of her egg roll and smiling.

SOMETHING TO BLOG ABOUT

The foot fetish kid was back at his usual computer, looking at all those feet again. I tried to distract myself during the tutoring session by imagining what the foot fetish kid is like away from his computer. Maybe he has a whole shrine to feet in his room. Like how I have all of my favorite actors taped all over my bedroom walls, maybe he has pictures of feet instead. And pillows shaped like feet that he cuddles up to every night.

But even those thoughts didn't do much to amuse me.

"SO HOW DID IT GO YESTERDAY?" KEISHA asked in homeroom. "I wanted to call you, but I figured your mom wouldn't let me talk to you. When is your punishment over?"

"Friday." I opened my chemistry textbook and stared down at the text. "You were wrong. He has no interest in me."

"Did he tell you that?" Keisha asked.

"No, but he didn't exactly seem eager to say that he *does* like me."

Keisha pushed her hair behind her ear and leaned toward me. "What happened?"

I told her everything, from the time I entered the library until we left that afternoon. I told her how I had spilled my guts to him and how the only thing he had to say in return was, "I'm sorry."

"Not one word about me being different from other girls or liking me," I finished. "Nothing. Just 'I'm sorry.'"

Keisha pressed her lips together in a tight line.

"What?" I asked, scowling.

"He likes you!" Keisha exclaimed. "You've scared him off with your freak-out. How was he supposed to tell you that he likes you when you already ran away once and then told him you weren't interested?"

I laughed. "Seth Jacobs isn't afraid of anything, least of all me."

"Open your eyes!" Keisha exclaimed. Other kids in our homeroom turned to look back at her, but she ignored them.

Like I'd really take *her* advice. She couldn't even see that Roger was her secret admirer. He knew everything about her. He always bought her movie ticket when we went out. He made me sit in the back of his car so she could sit up front next to him. His screen name was ZeppelinGuy. Earth to Keisha!

While I carried my tray across the cafeteria during lunch, I saw Roger standing by the snack machine on the other side of the room. He was in deep conversation with Seth.

"When did *they* become friends?" I asked, nodding toward Roger and Seth as I sat down.

Keisha turned around to look at them. "They're probably talking about you." She took a bite of her cheeseburger and then glanced at me.

"What?" I asked.

"Aren't you curious as to what they're talking about?"

I was, but I wasn't going anywhere near Seth to find out. "No." I opened my milk carton and began eating my sloppy joe.

"Speaking of Roger, have you noticed anything weird about him lately?" Keisha asked.

I nearly choked on my sandwich. "No," I said, between coughs.

"Something's going on with him," she said. "I saw him in the halls after every class yesterday, when I used to see him only twice a day. And we don't even have that many classes near each other."

"Maybe he's getting some exercise," I suggested. "You know, walking between classes."

"Or maybe . . ." Keisha began.

"What?" I asked.

Keisha shook her head, her curls bouncing. "Nothing.

It's just a dumb idea I had." She glanced toward Roger again, a strange look on her face.

At that moment, Seth and Roger went their separate ways. Roger sauntered over to our table and sat down.

"Hey, guys," he greeted us. He took a fry from my tray and stuffed it in his mouth.

"Spill it," I told him.

Roger blinked. "What?"

"What were you and Seth talking about?"

"Nothing," Roger said, shrugging.

"It didn't look like nothing," I told him.

"He's miserable over you."

I rolled my eyes. "Yeah, he really looks miserable."

Roger stood, brushing his hands on his jeans. "Don't believe me then. I'll see you guys later."

I glared at Roger as he left the room and spotted Seth seated at a table near the door, eating an ice-cream sandwich. He didn't look too miserable to me. He was probably daydreaming about some perfect girl with no confidence issues and who liked all the same music he did and didn't burn her hair.

Why would he ever want me when he could have Angel or anyone else at Yeardley?

SOMETHING TO BLOG ABOUT

Angel's getting me suspended has not caused her to ease up on tormenting me. If anything, it's getting worse. It used to be that Angel only did things to me every once in a while, like whenever she was bored. But now I can expect something from her every single day. Today she spilled a cup of ice water on my back in the cafeteria. Yesterday she stepped hard on my foot as she passed my desk in chemistry.

Every time I look at her, I can see the gears in her brain working as she tries to think of what she can do to me next. And my mom is not helping things at all! What does it take to get through to her and Mr. Rivera? Angel and I cannot peacefully coexist in the same room.

My life is a complete disaster these days. First Seth, now this . . .

MOM ARRIVED HOME EARLY THAT AFTER-
noon. She lugged in two armfuls of grocery bags and
deposited them on the counter.

"What are you doing now?" I asked. "And what is all of
that?"

"*That* is dinner," Mom said. "Manny called me at work
today. He wants us to try a nice dinner together again. He
thought maybe there was too much pressure last time, with
the long wait and buildup, so he figures that surprising
Angel might turn out better."

"I don't think Angel is the type who likes surprises," I
said. "And neither am I. I need time to prepare myself to face
her. You can't just tell me five minutes before we leave."

"We're not leaving." Mom began opening bags and

pulling cartons from them. "Manny and Angel are coming here."

"*Here?*" I repeated. "You invited Her Royal Nastiness to my home?"

"It's my home, too," Mom reminded me. She opened one carton to reveal a golden rotisserie chicken. "I bought these from the grocery store's deli. Does it look like I might have cooked it?"

"Only to someone who hasn't eaten your cooking her whole life." I nodded toward the packages and bags. "You'd better get rid of all of those," I said as I turned around. "I'm going to my room. Don't come get me when they arrive."

"I want you dressed nicely!" Mom called after me.

But instead of getting dressed, I sat down at my computer and opened my email. I started typing a long message to Keisha about how delusional my mom was. Couldn't Mom and Mr. Rivera get it through their heads that Angel and I were not the least bit interested in getting to know each other?

Just as I finished my letter, I heard the doorbell ring.

"Libby!" Mom called. "Please come out and greet our guests!"

I rolled my eyes, but I clicked Send and left my email

open in case I got a second to check for new messages during dinner.

Mr. Rivera was all smiles when I entered the living room, but Angel already looked as if she were in a foul mood. She stood a step behind her father, making a face as she took in her first glimpse of my home.

"*This* is where you live?" She looked around the room as she stepped inside. "It explains so much about you, Elizabeth."

"Like what?" I snapped.

"Why don't we go ahead and eat?" Mom suggested before Angel could respond. She smiled at all of us, but I could see that she was very nervous. She clasped her hands together in front of herself, then unfolded them and reached up to play with her earring. She had changed out of her scrubs and into a nice dress, though not as formal as the black one she'd worn on Saturday.

"You already have everything done?" Mr. Rivera asked as we walked into our kitchen. We didn't have a separate dining room and the kitchen itself was pretty small, so there wasn't a lot of room to move around. The four of us sat down at the round table, Angel seated directly across from me.

"Is this a kitchen or a closet?" Angel asked. She leaned forward and sniffed at the food spread out before us. "That looks—"

"Delicious," her father interrupted. He stared at Angel for a moment, then turned back to Mom and smiled. "This all looks delicious. I don't know how you did it on such short notice."

I stared down at my plate to hide my smirk.

"Oh, it was nothing," Mom said, waving a hand. "I left work a little early so I'd have time to get everything ready." She picked up a bowl of beans and offered them to Angel. "Would you like some green beans?"

Angel opened her mouth, but her father stared at her again, his face creased into a dark scowl. Angel took the bowl silently and spooned some beans onto her plate.

"Want some, Elizabeth?" Angel asked, smiling as she offered the bowl across the table.

I hadn't seen her spit into it or anything, so it seemed safe to take. But just as my fingers touched the bowl, Angel let go. The beans clattered back to the table, narrowly missing the plate of biscuits. Luckily, the bowl didn't tip over and only a few beans spilled out.

"Oops," Angel said. "I thought you had it."

I glared at her, but said, "No problem, Angelina. I'm a bit clumsy sometimes."

Mr. Rivera cleared his throat. "So, Libby," he said, "is anything exciting happening at school lately?"

I shrugged. "Same old, same old."

"What about your lovers' spat with Seth?" Angel asked.

Like I really wanted to talk about my boy problems with Angel's father!

"There was no spat," I said.

"Who's Seth?" Mr. Rivera asked.

"Just a boy at school that Libby likes," Mom told him. "But he doesn't seem to be as interested in her as she is in him."

"Mom!" I exclaimed, gripping my fork in my fist. "Why don't you just tell the whole world already?"

"Aww," Angel cooed. "Poor little Elizabeth. Want me to have a talk with him? After all, he is one of my *best* friends." She grinned at me evilly. I could imagine what kind of talk she'd like to have with Seth.

"No, thank you, Angelina," I told her, forcing a smile. "I think you do enough *talking* with the other guys in school."

Angel glared at me, but her father didn't seem to pick up on it.

"Well, this boy must not be worth your time, Libby," he said. "What boy wouldn't want a nice young lady like you?"

Ew. I did not need my mom's boyfriend trying to make me feel better about myself.

Angel turned her glare toward her father, but he kept eating his chicken and didn't look at her.

"Do you have a boyfriend, Angel?" Mom asked.

"No one special," Angel answered. I knew she wouldn't say anything about just how many boyfriends she had in front of her father.

"What's so funny, Libby?" Mom asked when she saw my smirk.

I wiped my mouth with my napkin. "Nothing at all."

We ate in silence for several moments. Homer slinked into the room, but stayed a safe distance from the table so that Angel couldn't taint him with her touch. Even animals know evil when they see it.

"What is that thing?" Angel asked, pointing her fork toward Homer.

"My cat," I answered.

"His name is Homer," Mom told her.

"He looks like a bowling ball on toothpicks," Angel said. "You ever heard of diet cat food?"

"You ever heard of being nice when you're in someone else's home?" I snapped.

"Enough!" Mom shouted. She gripped her napkin in her fist, her knuckles white. "Can we please have a nice meal together? Just once?"

Angel didn't say a word, so I said, "Fine with me."

Mom and Mr. Rivera exchanged a long, silent look.

I felt kind of bad for my mom and Angel's dad. They were trying so hard, forcing us to do things together. They had been happy all those months when it was just the two of them. Then they tried to include Angel and me in their happiness, and what did we do? Ripped each other's hair out and traded insults over dinner.

I really was a terrible daughter. Maybe not as terrible as Angel, but I was pretty high up there on the list of Worst Daughters Ever.

Mom frowned at her plate as she picked at her food. I looked away, trying to ignore the sudden twinge of guilt that spread through me. But even when I wasn't looking at her, I could still feel my mom's sadness.

If my mom really liked this guy, I could *attempt* to get along with Angel. It would take every bit of willpower I had, but I would try . . . for my mom.

When we had finished eating, Mom suggested we all

play a board game. We went to the living room, Mom and Mr. Rivera already laughing together, me trying to be optimistic, and Angel dragging along behind wearing a dark scowl. Even Homer followed us. When I sat down in one of the armchairs, he jumped into my lap and stared at Angel from his perch.

We decided on Trivial Pursuit, which I was pretty good at. But Mr. Rivera was great, winning three games in a row. He didn't even try to act dumb and let Mom or me win, which earned my respect. Angel, however, didn't attempt to answer any questions. She sat and stared at the wall.

I rubbed Homer's head while he purred and continued to stare at Angel.

Finally, Angel cried out, "Is that cat possessed? Make him stop staring at me."

Mom and Mr. Rivera looked up from the game, Mom holding a card in her hand.

"What is wrong now?" Mr. Rivera asked. I could hear a hint of annoyance in his tone.

"Nothing," I said. Maybe if I tried to be nice, this night would end sooner. I turned Homer around so that he faced me. "Sorry, Angel."

"Whatever." Angel stood and looked around. "Do you

have a bathroom in this cave?" she asked no one in particular.

"Down the hall, first door on the left," Mom answered, trying to smile.

Angel didn't return the gesture. She grumbled to herself as she disappeared into the hall.

Mom and Mr. Rivera went back to the game. I rubbed Homer's belly and whispered, "Good boy," very quietly.

Some time later, I realized Angel had been gone for quite a while. It would have been so perfect if she had food poisoning, but I doubted that was her problem.

I lifted Homer from my lap and walked into the hall. I noticed the bathroom door was open and the light turned off. Farther down the hall, my bedroom light was on.

What did she think she was doing? I never said she could go into my room! And I certainly would never give her permission to! Just when I was trying to give her a chance, she goes snooping where she has no right to be.

I stomped down the hall. "Get out!" I demanded as I reached the door.

I had expected to see Angel buried in my closet or peeking into my dresser drawers, but she was sitting at my desk in front of my computer. She closed the window on the screen before I could see what had her attention.

"What are you doing?" I asked. I took a quick survey of my room to figure out if anything was out of place. I wasn't exactly neat, and things were scattered everywhere, so it was hard to tell.

Angel stood and shrugged. "I got bored, so I was checking my email." She smirked. "Nice room." She pointed to my shelf of stuffed animals on one wall. "How cute."

"I didn't say you could use my computer," I told her.

"Sorry. I figured you were so busy with board games and your demon cat in there, you wouldn't mind if I came back here for a minute."

I crossed my arms. "What were you doing?"

"I told you, checking my email. I can't help it if it takes me more than five seconds to do that. Unlike you, I actually have friends who want to contact me."

I pointed at the door. "Out," I said through clenched teeth.

"I'm already gone," Angel told me as she left the room.

SOMETHING TO BLOG ABOUT

● ABOUT
● RECENT POSTS

● SEPTEMBER
● OCTOBER

THURSDAY, OCTOBER 25, 2:11 PM
GOOD-BYE FOREVER

I will NEVER blog again.

189

WHEN I GOT TO SCHOOL THURSDAY morning, I didn't notice anything out of the ordinary. People had been looking at me a lot since the fight—actually, ever

since the hair-burning incident—so I'd kind of gotten used to it. As I stopped at my locker, I noticed a bunch of people standing in a corner laughing about something.

Keisha was late to school and missed homeroom, so I read over the next few pages in my chemistry book alone. Since I started tutoring Seth, my grades had also improved. Ms. Hoover had passed back a chemistry test the day before and I actually got a B plus. She told me she was very impressed with my improvement and hoped I'd do well on the midterm.

It wasn't until I reached first period that I got the sense that something was wrong. Roger stormed toward me. He looked angrier than the time I stole his Teenage Mutant Ninja Turtles action figures when we were kids.

"How *could* you?" he roared.

I blinked. "You'll have to be specific. How could I what?"

"Now Keisha will find out I'm her secret admirer! I'm not ready to tell her yet, and not this way!"

I held up my hands. "Roger, seriously, I have no clue what you're talking about."

"I trusted you . . ." Roger said as he stomped away.

As I walked into my class, I noticed that many people seemed to be staring at me. When I passed a group of the popular kids, they laughed louder than usual.

People snuck glances at me all through first period. I raced out of the room and toward Keisha's locker as soon as the bell rang. She was closing it as I reached her.

"Is it my imagination," I asked, "or has everyone in this school gone completely crazy?"

"I don't know," Keisha said. The muscles in her face twitched and her mouth was tight. "Should I just kick everyone's butt? That's all I ever talk about, right? I'm just a mental case who wants to kick everyone's butt."

I took a step back. "Okay, it seems you've gone crazy along with everyone else. I'm going to back away slowly."

"That's probably the smart thing to do," Keisha said in a low tone. She reached into her backpack and pulled out a crumpled piece of paper. "You can have this back."

I stared at the paper she'd hurled to the floor after she stalked away. What was with everyone?

I picked up the paper and unfolded it, scanning over the words. SOMETIMES I THINK KEISHA IS A MENTAL CASE WAITING TO BE UNLEASHED. My stomach plummeted to my toes and my entire body grew cold. I was reading one of the entries from my blog.

How had Keisha gotten it? I looked around the hall and saw people looking at me and whispering to their friends. Had they all read it, too?

After second period, I knew I was in trouble. I saw several of my blog entries posted on a bulletin board outside my classroom, and more printouts taped on lockers all down the hallway. Some were taped to the side of a water fountain. There were even a few covering the door to the cafeteria. Each page had the words LIBBY FAWCETT'S SECRET BLOG scribbled in pen across the top, above my blog title, SOMETHING TO BLOG ABOUT. People stood in front of the pages, pointing out passages to their friends.

I pushed through the crowd and ripped the papers down.

"Who did this?" I asked.

No one answered. The crowd dispersed to their classes, still laughing and glancing back at me.

My entries were all there. Everything I'd poured out into my blog was now posted for the entire school to see. It was like someone had split my chest open and laid my heart on a table for everyone to poke and inspect.

How could this have happened? I had made the blog private, I was sure of it. And I hadn't said a word about having a digital diary to anyone, not even to Keisha or Roger.

Who would do something like this?

"Read anything interesting lately, Elizabeth?" Angel sneered at me as she passed by.

Something clicked in my brain. Angel had been in my room. At my computer. And I had left my email open before dinner. The welcome message from the blog site popped into my head. My user name and password were listed in that email. I had never deleted it from my inbox in case I forgot my password.

I felt sick. My body began to shake and I thought

my legs would give out on me. I couldn't go to class. I couldn't face anyone or listen to their whispers and laughs. I couldn't watch Roger and Keisha shoot me angry glances.

And I couldn't bear to find out if Seth had read the entries.

What if he had read everything I had written about him? What if he knew how much I liked him?

I ran away and hid in the girls' bathroom near the band class. I sat in a stall and cried.

When the bell rang, I didn't go to my next class. I went to the library and snuck into the bathroom there.

What did I ever do to deserve this? I could *never* show my face in school again. I really meant it this time.

Finally, I gathered up enough courage to leave the bathroom and I stepped into the library's main room. As soon as I did, Seth cornered me.

"Came here to spill more secrets on that website?" he asked, his voice cold and even.

"I wasn't—"

Seth wouldn't let me finish. "Everything I told you—about me, about my mom—that was meant to remain between you and me. You've been telling the whole world about me through your blog?"

"It was a private diary," I said. "No one was ever supposed to see it."

"You put it on the Internet!" Seth shouted, his voice echoing off the shelves and around the silent room. "What did you think would happen?"

"I thought I could . . ." How could I have been so stupid? Leaving my email open . . . letting Angel out of sight the night before . . . Of course she couldn't resist.

No, this was the fault of my mother and Mr. Rivera. If they hadn't started dating, Angel would have never come to my home and snooped around on my computer.

Ms. Taylor approached us. "I'm afraid I'm going to have to ask you to quiet down," she said, scowling at both of us. "This is a library. Library voices, remember?" She sneered at us and went back to her desk.

"I thought you were different, Libby." Seth's eyes shone, as if they had filled with tears. "I thought finally I had found a girl who wasn't like anyone else in this school. Someone who didn't spread gossip. Someone I could talk to and be myself with."

I stared at the floor. A tear slipped down my cheek and landed on my shoe.

"You're just like the rest of them."

I couldn't listen anymore.

I ran out of the library and hid in the bathroom again, locked away in a stall. There were two girls in the stalls on either side of me, so I tried to stifle my sobs.

"Did you see that stuff that's been posted all over school?" one girl asked.

"Yeah," the other answered from her stall. "Can you believe all the things she wrote? She's so clueless."

"Who is that girl, anyway?" the first girl asked.

"You know, that one who burned her hair off and then got into a fight with Angel Rivera. I thought she was really cool after the fight, but did you read the entry about that day? She didn't even know it was coming. And then she whined about how unfair it was that she got suspended."

The toilets flushed and the girls left their stalls, laughing.

I wiped my eyes with some toilet paper.

I couldn't stay at school for the rest of the day. I couldn't look at all those people, knowing they'd read the personal things I had written.

People laughed as I walked down the hall, but I kept my gaze on the floor. When I made it out the front door, I walked across the lawn and crossed the street. Then I just started running.

• • •

Homer was happy to see me when I stepped into the silent apartment. I picked him up and buried my face in his fur.

"You're the only one who doesn't hate me, Homie," I told him. He started to purr.

Thursday, October 25, 8:36 PM

I can't blog anymore. I opened the website up earlier and tried to write something about what happened with Angel, but I couldn't. Every time I started to type, I'd think, "What if Angel finds out my password again?" I changed it as soon as I could, but with her you never know.

So I found this old notebook in my desk and decided to write in it. I can't just NOT write anymore. Even though Angel has ruined my life—I need to keep writing.

MOM CAME HOME AT TWO THIRTY. SHE looked relieved when she saw me lying on my bed.

"Libby!" she exclaimed. "What are you doing here? I got a call at work saying you haven't been to any of your classes since second period."

She stopped talking when I rolled over. As soon as she saw that I'd been crying, she sat on the bed next to me and pulled me into her arms.

"What happened?" she asked. "Is it that boy again?"

I wished it were just Seth and not the entire world.

"Everyone hates me," I said before I started crying again.

Mom held me, rocking me back and forth, and just let me cry. When my sobs had subsided, she asked, "Why does everyone hate you?"

I told her about the blog and about everything I had written. Then I told her about finding the pages of my blog posted all over the school.

"Now Keisha is mad because she said I made her look like a sociopath. Roger hates me because his secret has been revealed before he could do it himself. And Seth definitely hates me for telling everyone about his personal life. The rest of the school is just laughing at me and having a great time."

Mom sighed heavily. "You've really gotten yourself into a mess, haven't you?"

I sat up, pulling myself from her embrace. "This isn't my fault! It's Angel's. She posted my blog entries everywhere. And Angel would never have been in my room if you weren't dating her father!"

"You can't blame Manny and me for what happens between Angel and you," Mom said. "If you hadn't left your email open, Angel wouldn't have seen your username and password to get into your journal."

"What?"

I flopped down and buried my face in my pillows. "I can't believe you're taking Angel's side in this."

"I'm not," Mom told me. She reached over to rub my back, like she used to when I was little. "Angel had no right to post your personal writings all over the school. And she had no right to be in your room when she wasn't invited."

While Mom rubbed my back, I could almost believe that things would be okay again. Whenever Roger and I would fight over toys or some other silly thing when we were kids, Mom would sit next to me on my bed and rub my back and tell me it would be over soon. And back then, she was right.

But this time things wouldn't be over soon. Angel and her friends would never let me forget about this.

"Am I in trouble for leaving school without permission?" I asked. "Grounded for another week?"

"No," Mom said. "I think you've been through enough today. But next time, tell me where you'll be. I had no idea what might have happened to you when the school called me."

"Sorry."

Mom leaned over and rested her head on my shoulder. "I love you, Libby. Everything will be back to normal soon enough. I know it."

I wished I could believe that.

Friday, October 26, 12:14 PM

I didn't want to go to school this morning and I thought Mom would let me stay home. But she made me get out of bed and told me, "You can't hide from your problems forever. I raised you to be a strong woman . . . This will pass."

But will I have any friends once the rest of the school has stopped laughing at me? Keisha and Roger are SO mad. They wouldn't answer my IMs last night. And Seth didn't look at me even once in the halls today.

I guess Angel has gotten one thing she wanted out of this—Seth is all hers now.

WHILE I SAT AT A COMPUTER IN THE LIBRARY
during lunch, the foot fetish kid looked over at me and said,
"You're Libby, right?"

I wondered if he had read the things I'd written about
him and was now going to yell at me, too. "Yeah," I said,
cringing as I waited for the verbal onslaught.

"Your blog was hilarious," he told me. "I don't usually
read stuff like that, but someone in my math class had
some of the pages. You should be a professional writer."

I hadn't expected that at all, so I just said, "Thanks."

He smiled, then turned back to his pictures of feet.

After a few moments, I had to ask, "I'm sorry to
bother you, but I wanted to ask you about my blog.
Didn't you see the things I had written about you?"

The foot fetish kid nodded. "Yeah, I did."

"So you weren't upset?"

"Why should I be? I do look at pictures of feet. Although I don't have a foot fetish, I have a *shoe* fetish." He shrugged, grinning at me a moment before turning back to his computer.

My friends didn't speak to me at all that day. Roger wouldn't even look at me. Neither would Seth, for that matter. I kept sneaking glances at him during chemistry, but he just sat slumped at his desk and didn't look my way.

A lot of people still snickered at me, but not as many as the day before. Most of the popular kids were all talking about a party someone was having Saturday night.

Even Angel was too preoccupied to torment me. The county art show was the next afternoon at the community center, and I could hear her talk nonstop about it to Tara and Kim, who didn't look too interested.

But she couldn't resist opening her mouth as I walked out of class. "Aw, poor Elizabeth," Angel said. "What's the matter? Lost all your friends?"

I watched Keisha and Roger leave the room without speaking to me.

"Thanks for everything, Angel," I said. "Can I go now or is there a part of my life you haven't ruined yet?"

Angel tossed her hair over her shoulder. "Your mom must be pretty mad, huh?" she asked. "She probably hates me, right? And blames my father since, you know, he made me who I am."

"I have no idea what my mom's feelings regarding you are, but I doubt she blames your father. Sorry to disappoint you, Angel, but my mom loves him. She may even want to marry him someday. And whether you like it or not, there isn't a thing you or I can do about it. And you know what? I'd rather see my mom happy and with someone who truly loves her than break them up just because of you."

I realized as I walked away that everything I had said was true. I was happy my mom had found someone who really cared about her as much as Mr. Rivera seemed to. Even Angel couldn't make me take that away from her.

Friday, October 26, 5:14 PM

I waited in the library after school today, but Seth didn't show up. I didn't really expect him to, since he hadn't spoken to me all day, but I thought just maybe he'd give me a second chance. Apparently he's decided he doesn't even need—or doesn't want—my help in chemistry. I'm not even good enough to be his tutor.

I'm not grounded anymore. My first day of freedom, but I have nowhere to go and no one to hang out with. The only thing I have to look forward to tonight is watching TV with my cat. I lead such a thrilling life.

MOM HAD MADE PLANS TO GO OUT WITH some friends from work to see a movie that night, but I nearly had to push her out the door to get her to go.

"I feel bad about leaving you here alone," she said, playing with her earring. "Maybe I could go rent a movie instead, and we could pop some popcorn and have a night in together."

"No way." I grabbed her purse and shoved it into her arms. "You need a night out with your girlfriends. Go have fun, flirt with cute guys, talk too loud during the movie, do all those things you girls do when you get together. I'll be fine."

Mom hesitated again. "Are you sure?"

I waved my hands toward the door. "Go! You're going to be late!"

Mom blew a kiss to me as she closed the door behind her. Homer weaved between my legs, meowing up at me.

"Looks like it's just you and me," I told him. "What do you want to watch? Should I find a documentary on birds for you?"

I sat down on the couch and flipped through the channels, but there was nothing terribly interesting on.

The phone rang and I groaned as I got up to answer it.

"Hi, Libby! Is your mother home?" I recognized Mr. Rivera's voice.

"No, I'm sorry, she went out with her friends. Do you want me to give her a message?"

"Oh," Mr. Rivera said, sounding disappointed. "No, that's okay. I'm in Asheville right now. I had to come here to meet with some people about a case I'm working on. And I thought I'd give your mother a call since I won't be seeing her this weekend."

My forehead creased in confusion. "You're in Asheville? But what about Angel's art show?"

There was a moment of silence and then Mr. Rivera said, "What about it?"

"Well, Asheville is six hours away. You can't just drop by the Yeardley Community Center between meetings to see her artwork."

"I realize that, Libby," Mr. Rivera said. "Angel understands that I have to work. She doesn't care whether I'm there or not."

I remembered the way Angel had tensed when the little girl in the bookstore asked if Mr. Rivera was coming to the show and I remembered the look in Angel's eyes when Mom and I had dinner at the Riveras' and her father mentioned going to one of my track meets some day.

Something wasn't right and Mr. Rivera didn't seem to get it.

A little voice in my head begged me to leave it alone—it wasn't any of my business and Angel could cry about her daddy not loving her if she wanted and I didn't care . . .

But another voice said that Mom and Mr. Rivera had made it my business when they decided Angel and I should get to know each other. Like it or not, I had learned something about Angel, something she probably had never told anyone. And that something was that Angel Rivera needed attention and support just like any other teenager.

"Um, Mr. Rivera," I said, twisting a loose thread from my shirt around my finger, "please don't get angry at me for saying this, but I think you don't know your daughter."

I paused. Mr. Rivera was silent, except for the steady sound of his breathing.

"You're the only parent Angel has. This show is really important to her. It's an all-county show and only the best get in. Do you realize only four artists from our school were chosen to have their work in the exhibition? And Angel was one of them. That is a *huge* deal. I know if it were a track meet and I was one of only four from my school who got to compete, I'd be so excited and—"

"What exactly are you trying to say, Libby?" Mr. Rivera interrupted. He sounded slightly annoyed, and for a moment I considered backing down.

But maybe if Mr. Rivera gave her what she needed from him, Angel would back off and stop tormenting me. Could it be that Angel Rivera was just as insecure about life as I was?

And maybe hell would freeze over.

Whatever. I had started this. I couldn't stop it until I had my say.

"I'm just saying that you should go to the art show," I told him. "Maybe you could put aside your work for one afternoon and be there for Angel. She may pretend she doesn't care if you're there, but trust me, she does. My mom goes to almost all of my track meets. Even if I don't win, she's there."

"I have meetings all day tomorrow," Mr. Rivera said. "I've been trying to track this witness down for months. I can't just cancel at the last minute. I have a demanding job—"

"And my mom has a demanding job, too," I said. "And friends and dates and a life outside of me. But she makes time to let me know she loves me."

We were silent for a moment. Then Mr. Rivera said, "Thank you for your concern, Libby. I'm sure Angel will do well at the show and won't even notice my absence. Tell your mother I called and I'll try to call her again Sunday when I get home."

I sighed, knowing everything I'd said had gone in one ear and out the other. "I will. Bye, Mr. Rivera."

"Good-bye, Libby," he said gruffly before hanging up.

SATURDAY, OCTOBER 27, 2:07 PM

I should learn to keep my mouth shut and stay out of things that aren't any of my concern. What possessed me to worry about ANGEL'S feelings anyway? After what she did to me, I wish she'd just disappear. What do I care if her dad ignores her? She can go cry in the corner like I've been doing since yesterday, thanks to her.

It doesn't matter anyway. Mr. Rivera didn't seem to be worried about what I had to say and whatever problems he and Angel have aren't going to be solved by me.

"ARE YOU SURE YOU DON'T WANT TO GO?" Mom asked for the twentieth time Saturday afternoon.

"I'm sure." I flopped down on the couch and propped my feet on the armrest. "I don't think Angel would really want me there anyway."

Mom smoothed my hair back and leaned down to kiss my forehead. "I'm going, whether she wants me there or not. She needs someone cheering her on."

"Yeah, well, just don't let her find out about any secret diaries you may have."

Mom laughed as she walked out the door, leaving me alone in the apartment.

No way would I ever go to Angel's art show. She'd probably trip me and cause me to break something. Or maybe I'd be unable to control my anger and end up throwing sculptures at her.

It had been two days since the blog incident and still none of my friends were talking to me. The phone hadn't rung, except for telemarketers and Mr. Rivera's call the night before. My inbox was empty, not even spammers had sent me anything. They, too, were giving me the silent treatment.

Everyone hated me. I felt tears welling up in my eyes again. I thought I had done all the crying that was possible for one person to do already.

Rubbing at my eyes with the backs of my hands, I got up and walked to the kitchen. I opened the refrigerator and stared inside for a moment, but I didn't really want anything to eat or drink.

Homer sat on the floor at my feet, watching me with his big green eyes. I scooped him into my arms and buried my face in his fur.

"I guess I really messed up this time," I told him. "I'm used to bad things happening in my life, but it's never been anything as big as this. The truth is, I never expected anyone to ever read what I wrote. Angel shouldn't have ever found it."

The phone rang, making me jump and startle Homer

so that he dug his claws into my leg. I limped toward the phone, rubbing my wounds.

"Hello?"

There was a lot of static, but I could hear someone say, "Hello? Libby?"

"Mr. Rivera?" I pressed the phone closer to my ear, trying to hear over the noise.

"Yes . . . Is . . . mom there?"

"My mom? No, she went to Angel's show."

"Really? Good. I'm . . . don't know . . ."

"You're breaking up," I said. "I can barely hear you through the static. Where are you?"

"I'm . . . half hour . . . Yeardley," Mr. Rivera said. "I . . . back from Asheville to . . . the show . . . Car . . . overheated. I'm . . . middle of nowhere."

I stood up straight, gripping the phone tight. "You came back to go to the show?" I did it! I had told Mr. Rivera what I thought and he had actually listened to me!

"Yes, but . . . car . . ."

"Oh! Your car overheated!" I said, the words finally sinking in. I had to think fast. Mr. Rivera needed to get to the show before it was over or everything I had said and his drive back all would have been for nothing. "Okay, where are you?"

"Highway seventy," Mr. Rivera said. "Sutton's Grove . . . Call a cab . . . tow truck."

"No, they'll never understand you with all that static," I said. "I'll come get you. Stay right there!"

"But—"

I hung up before Mr. Rivera had a chance to protest. There was no time to waste arguing. Adrenaline pumped through my body, filling me with the need to get moving.

But I didn't have a car. I didn't have a license! And I couldn't exactly walk all the way to Sutton's Grove and then back with Mr. Rivera.

I tapped my fingers on my chin. Mom was probably already at the community center. And of course she's still in the twentieth century without a cell phone. And I had no money to pay for a taxi.

I had to call someone. Everyone was still mad at me, but I had to try.

"Hi, Uncle Matt," I greeted Roger's father when he answered.

"Hey, Libs." Uncle Matt was a great guy and loved to make people laugh. Any other time, I would have been happy to chat with him, but not right then.

"Is Roger home?" I asked.

"Yep, he is. You want to speak to him?"

"Yes, but don't tell him it's me on the phone. He's a little mad at me right now and probably wouldn't answer if he knew who it was."

"Oh, sure thing, Libs. Just a second."

I waited while Uncle Matt went to get Roger. After a moment, I heard Roger say, "Hello?"

I took in a deep breath and began talking fast before he could hang up. "Roger, it's Libby, but please don't hang up. No one else will talk to me and I'm sorry for the blog and I will make it up to you, I promise, but I really, *really* need your help right now."

I stopped to catch my breath and waited to see if he'd hung up. I heard only silence.

"You still there?" I asked.

"Yeah," Roger answered.

Thank you!

"Angel is in the art show at the community center today and my mom has already left. Mr. Rivera just called me and his car broke down near Sutton's Grove. I need someone to drive me out there to pick him up and take him to the show."

Roger was silent for a moment. Then he said, "Why do you care about Angel and her art show? After what she did to you?"

"I know," I said, twisting the phone cord around my fingers. "But I keep thinking about seeing her in the bookstore that night. She wants her father to be at that show. And who knows? She could be my stepsister one day, so I'd like to try to make things better between us if I can."

"Angel as your stepsister? That's a frightening thought."

I laughed a little. It was a good sign that Roger was making jokes. "I know, but our parents seem pretty serious about each other. So . . . will you drive me out there?"

Roger sighed. "How long will it take?"

"Only about an hour. We'll get him, take him to the show, and then you can go home."

"Okay," Roger said. "I'll be over there in a minute."

"Thank you!" I cried into the phone. "And I meant what I said. I'll make everything up to you. I don't know how, but I will. I'll fix everything."

"Yeah," Roger said before hanging up.

When Roger arrived, I dashed out to his car so he wouldn't have to come up to the apartment.

"Thank you," I said as I got into the car.

Roger nodded but didn't speak.

"Has Keisha said anything about the secret admirer thing?" I asked.

"No," Roger answered. "But I've been avoiding her as much as I can."

"Is she talking to you?"

"Yeah, about everything else. But not the secret admirer thing." He fiddled with the knobs on his car's radio. "Maybe she's not interested in me and doesn't know how to tell me."

"That can't be it," I said. "Keisha likes you and she likes spending time with you. I'm sure if she knew you were her secret admirer, she'd be thrilled."

I had to make everything right somehow.

"I feel horrible. These last three days have been the absolute worst of my life. My friends hate me and everyone else in school thinks I'm a joke." I was dangerously close to crying again. "I hate myself for hurting everyone. I never thought that what I had written could be used against me or anyone else."

Roger reached over and laced his fingers with mine. "It'll be all right, Libs," he told me. "And I don't hate you. So you ruined my secret admirer thing? Big deal. Now that it's out there in the open, you've saved me the trouble of having to figure out a way to do it myself."

I wiped my eyes with my free hand. "Really?"

"Yeah," Roger answered.

"Well, I promise to talk to her. Even though she's not exactly willing to talk to me."

"Maybe you'd better focus on one thing at a time," Roger said.

We rode the rest of the way mostly in silence, making small talk every now and then. I kept thinking about Keisha and Roger and, of course, about Seth.

I wasn't very optimistic that Seth would ever speak to me again, but I had to make things right with my friends. If I had lost any chance with him for good, I needed my friends to help me move on.

"There he is!" I exclaimed, pointing at the highway across the median, where I saw Mr. Rivera's car pulled to the shoulder, the hood opened. Roger turned around at the next available place and we pulled to a stop.

Mr. Rivera got out of his car, closed the hood, and then walked over to Roger's car and leaned down to look at us.

"You really didn't have to come get me, Libby," he said. But he smiled and then climbed into the backseat.

"It's no problem," I said. "Right, Roger?"

Roger nodded. "Of course. It's nice to meet you, Mr. Rivera. I'm Libby's cousin, Roger Fawcett."

"Oh, yes," Mr. Rivera said. "Maura has told me about you. You're her brother's oldest, right?"

"Yes, sir." Roger pulled back onto the highway and we were on our way back toward Yeardley.

I turned around to look at Mr. Rivera and said, "I thought you weren't coming back for the show."

"I didn't intend to," Mr. Rivera said. He ran a hand over his black hair, smoothing down the bits the wind had mussed. "But then, well, someone changed my mind." He winked.

"I'm glad you came back. I knew my mom wouldn't date a bad guy."

"I'm happy I passed your test."

And Mr. Rivera wasn't a bad guy. As we drove back to Yeardley, he told us funny stories about Angel when she was a kid and then he tried to tell us a few jokes. They were terrible and I didn't understand half of them, but Roger and I laughed politely anyway.

When we arrived at the community center, the parking lot was pretty full. A huge sign in front of the building advertised the county show and competition, bragging, FEATURING THE BEST ARTISTS IN THE AREA!

Angel was one of those best artists. That was kind of surreal.

"You don't have to stay," I told Roger as I climbed out of the car. "I'll get a ride home with my mom."

Roger turned off the ignition and looked at his watch. "I'll come in. It's not like I have anything else to do today. And I'm actually curious to see Angel's work." He looked at his watch again before he got out of the car, then took a long look around the parking lot.

"What's wrong with you?" I asked.

"Nothing," Roger said. "Let's go in."

We entered the building together, looking around at the people milling about by various paintings and sculptures. A small group of people in suits, wearing ribbons that read JUDGE, walked around all of the exhibits, whispering among themselves, writing on the clipboards they carried.

I spotted my mom, who stood awkwardly, a smile plastered across her face even though her forehead was wrinkled into a scowl. Next to her was Angel, arms crossed and looking bored, next to a black pedestal.

Mom saw me and started to wave, but then she saw Mr. Rivera and broke into a huge smile. "Libby! Manny!"

she exclaimed when we drew close. "What are you doing here?"

Saying that I had come to support Angel would have sounded stupid coming from my mouth. Besides, I didn't want Angel to think I pitied her or anything.

So I shrugged and said, "We had to go pick this guy up." I nodded at Mr. Rivera. "He was getting ready to hitchhike back to town after his car broke down."

"Luckily, Libby and Roger rescued me." Mr. Rivera turned to his daughter and smiled. "I couldn't miss your show, baby girl."

Angel looked stunned, as if she had no idea what to do or say. Mr. Rivera seemed apprehensive for a moment, but then the tiniest trace of a smile flashed across Angel's face and he relaxed a bit.

"Is this your piece?" Roger asked Angel, turning toward the black pedestal.

I turned to get a good look, too.

And then I froze, unable to think of a thing to say.

It was a small sculpture, but *what* exactly it was a sculpture of, I had no clue. It was orange, with curves on one side, a jagged edge on the other, and a hole in the top left corner.

"Pretty cool," Roger said.

Angel looked at me, smirking, and I knew she was waiting for me to say something.

"Um," I stammered, trying to come up with something nice. "I like . . . the shape . . . of the . . . the, um . . ."

What was that thing?

Angel laughed. "It's abstract art, Elizabeth. It's not supposed to be anything."

"Oh, good," I said, relieved. "I mean, that's what I thought. Abstract art, exactly."

Angel rolled her eyes. "You are clueless."

"It looks great," Mr. Rivera told his daughter, reaching his arm around her to hug her to his side. "First-place material."

Angel actually blushed. "Thanks."

Mom leaned toward me and whispered, "Thank you, Libby. She's been a total grouch until now."

"No problem," I whispered back.

"Hey, Libby," said a voice behind me.

I froze in place, unable to turn around. I squeezed my eyes shut, praying that I wasn't imagining things.

Mom poked my side and I opened my eyes, forcing myself to face him.

Seth.

"What are you doing here?" The question tumbled from my mouth before I had a chance to remember he hated me.

"I called him," Roger said. "You two need to talk."

Seth buried his hands in his pockets, avoiding my gaze.

"Oh, please," Angel said, making a face. "Just jump each other's bones and get it over with. And go away before the judges get here. I don't want them thinking you two are part of my work and calling it pathetic."

"I guess we could go outside," I said, keeping my gaze on the floor while I spoke. "I mean, if you want to."

Seth nodded. "Yeah, okay. Nice sculpture, Angel."

I was very aware of Seth walking a step behind me as I made my way toward the front doors. Once we were outside, I leaned against a brick wall and wrapped my arms around myself to keep warm.

Seth just stood and stared into the distance.

He hated me and would probably hate me forever. I could get over it.

Eventually.

Finally, I couldn't stand the silence any longer.

"I'm sorry—" I said at the same time Seth said, "Libby, I—"

We both stopped, glancing at each other quickly and then looking away.

"You go first," I said.

"No, you go ahead," Seth told me.

Might as well get it over with.

"I'm really, really sorry about the blog," I said. "I never meant for anyone else to ever read it. I had it password-protected and I thought that was enough to keep it private. But then Angel went into my room and read my email and . . ."

I waved a hand into the air. "You know what happened after that. I'm so sorry."

"I know," Seth said. "And I'm sorry about what I said to you on Thursday."

I shrugged. "It's okay. A lot of people have said some not-so-nice things to me lately. I deserved it."

Seth sighed, running a hand through his hair. "It's not okay. I'm a jerk. A huge, stupid jerk. Not just about the blog, but about the way I've acted around you."

"That's not true," I said. "I realize that you just needed a tutor. I was stupid to ever think anything different . . ."

"Libby," Seth said in an annoyed tone. "Can I talk for a minute?"

I closed my mouth and nodded.

"I was angry about my personal life becoming part of the gossip at school," Seth told me. The muscles in his jaw twitched and he twisted his hands together as he spoke. "And I was mad at Angel for posting pages from your blog, but I was even more angry with you for writing it down in the first place. I felt like I could share anything with you and be exactly who I am, not who everyone else thought I should be. I've never told anyone else about my mom abandoning me—not even Angel, and she's the closest thing to a best friend I've ever had. Until I got to know you. I felt like you wouldn't judge me. And . . . I like being with you."

I waited for whatever he was going to say next. That he didn't feel that way anymore, that he couldn't move past it. I was willing to accept it if he never wanted to see me again.

"But I messed that all up," he said. "It killed me when you ran away crying yesterday because *I* did that to you. I made you cry."

After a moment, I found my voice. "It's okay," I whispered.

"No, it's not." Seth stepped forward and took my hands in his. "I like you, Libby, a lot. That day I said you were cute and you ran away, I figured that meant you didn't feel the same about me and were too uncomfortable to say so.

I didn't want to ruin our friendship, so I didn't mention it again. I've liked you all this time, but I didn't know how to tell you, so I asked you to tutor me.

"I took your blog entries home and read them. I saw all the things you'd written about me. I hated myself for telling you that you were a terrible person. Because you're not."

I was dumbfounded.

"Anyway," he said as he dropped my hands and stepped back, "I'm sorry. When I first saw the blog I thought you were like the other girls in school, as fake and vapid as they are. But I realized that I have it backward. I'm like them and you are the one who's better than all of us." He gave me a sad smile and then started down the steps toward the parking lot.

"Seth?" My voice was barely above a whisper, but he turned around.

I walked down the steps to him. And then I did something I didn't know I could do. A month ago I wouldn't have dared, I would have sat silently forever and let the chance slip away. But after the last few weeks I'd had, I was more afraid of what would happen if I didn't go for it than what would happen if I did.

So I went for it.

I, Libby Fawcett, kissed Seth Jacobs in the parking lot of the Yeardley Community Center.

And he kissed me back.

When we came up for air, Seth said, "So let me get this straight. You don't hate me?"

"I never did." I looked down at my feet. "I'm sorry the things I wrote got posted all over school."

He put a finger under my chin and tilted my face toward his. It was just like those old romantic movies, when the guy looks deeply into the girl's eyes and professes his love to her. Except that they never stood outside a community center while people were coming and going and watching them with mild amusement.

"I think we've both done some dumb things lately," he told me. "Let's just start over, okay?"

I smiled. "Okay."

"I guess we should go back inside and see if Angel wins," Seth said.

"One question first," I said. "Do you know what Angel's sculpture is?"

"Abstract art, right?"

I threw my hands up in the air. "Why am I the only one who doesn't know that?"

I turned to go back inside. As we walked up the steps, Seth reached over and took my hand in his.

I shivered, tingles of excitement spreading throughout my body.

When we made it back to Angel's exhibit, the little girl from the bookstore had joined them. She beamed up at Angel with admiration as she talked.

"Hi," the girl said when she noticed Seth and me. "I'm Holly."

"We both take classes here at the community center," Angel explained. She smiled down at Holly and mussed her hair. "This kid sticks to me like glue."

I smiled. "I'm Libby, Angel's . . . um . . ." I couldn't say friend. Angel and I probably would never exactly be friends. "I guess I'm Angel's future stepsister. Possibly."

Seth said hello to Holly and introduced himself to Mr. Rivera and my mom. After the introductions, my mom pulled me aside and whispered, "Future stepsister?"

I grinned and shrugged. "You and Mr. Rivera really seem to be in love. I figured it's only a matter of time before you start talking about the M word."

"We thought you and Angel didn't want that."

I put my hands on her shoulders and looked into her eyes. "Mom, do you love him?"

Mom's expression softened. "Yes. Very much."

I glanced at Seth over her shoulder. Just the sight of him made me happy. I could understand how my mother felt.

I gave Mom's shoulders a squeeze. "Then go for it."

"Here come the judges!" Holly exclaimed, bouncing up and down and tugging on Angel's arm. "They're bringing— Oh, my gosh! Angel!"

The judges stopped in front of Angel's sculpture. A man with a thick gray beard smiled as he attached a red ribbon to the pedestal. "Congratulations, Miss Rivera," he said, shaking Angel's hand. "We look forward to seeing more work from you in the future."

When the judges had all given their congratulations and moved on, Mr. Rivera scooped Angel into his arms and twirled her around. "Second place!" he exclaimed.

"Congratulations, Angel," Mom said. Roger and Seth added their congratulations, too.

When her father put her down, Angel looked at me, smirking slightly. I wanted to say something mean, like, "Too bad you're not good enough for first place." But Mr. Rivera's face shone with pride and my mom smiled lovingly at him. I couldn't bring myself to ruin this moment for them.

So I said, "Congratulations."

Angel looked at me again, as if she were considering saying something sarcastic in response. But after a moment she shrugged, said, "Thanks," and turned back to Holly, who was still bouncing around excitedly.

"I need to get going," Roger told me.

"Yeah, me, too," Seth said. "Did you want to stay here or come with me?"

"I'll go with you," I said, making a face. "I don't know how much longer I can be nice if I stay within five feet of Angel."

I told my mom I was leaving and then walked outside with Seth and Roger. Seth held my hand again, as if he were afraid to let me out of his reach. That was perfectly fine with me.

Roger gave us a half-smile when he reached his car. "Well, at least one good thing has come out of this," he said.

I suddenly remembered Roger and Keisha and the secret admirer thing. I had promised Roger I would fix everything and I was determined to keep that promise.

"Meet me at Pizza 'N More at noon tomorrow," I told him.

"Why?" Roger asked.

I had the hint of a plan in my head, but I didn't want to say anything yet in case it all fell through. "Just be there, okay?"

"Sure, why not? It's not like I have a demanding schedule." Roger waved as he got into his car.

Seth and I walked across the parking lot to his Jeep. He opened the door for me and bowed low. "Your chariot awaits."

I giggled as I climbed in. Seth shut the door and then jogged around the car to the driver's side. He got in, started the ignition, and then looked at me.

"Where to?" he asked.

I felt as if I might explode from happiness at any moment. I had thought after Angel posted my blog entries all over school that I'd never feel like this again. But at that very moment, I didn't care about Angel or the problems that I still hadn't fixed. I only cared that Seth was seated next to me and finally the truth was out and we both knew how we felt about each other.

"Anywhere," I answered.

Sunday, October 28, 11:28 AM

I slept longer than I meant to this morning, but I have a good excuse. I lay in bed for hours last night, reliving every single kiss Seth and I shared yesterday. Which was a lot.

I'm still exhausted, but I forced myself up. I took a record shower, in and out in three minutes, put down food for Homer, and I'm about to race out the door. I have some serious work to do.

I RAN ALL THE WAY TO KEISHA'S HOUSE, which, thankfully, wasn't that far from my apartment. Still, her mom found me bent over, trying to catch my breath when she answered the door.

"Libby!" Mrs. Jones exclaimed, taking my hand and ushering me into the house. "Sit down. Have you been running?"

"Hi, Mrs. Jones," I managed to say. "Is Keisha here?"

"In her room," her mom told me, "but—"

I flew up the stairs before she could say anything else. Keisha's door was closed, but I swung it open anyway.

Keisha lay on her bed reading a magazine, but looked up when the door opened. She scowled when she saw it was me.

"Ever heard of knocking?" She flipped the page in her magazine with so much force it ripped in half.

"I don't have time to knock," I told her.

I knew there was only one way to make Keisha accept my apology.

I dropped to my knees and crawled to the side of her bed. "I am completely, totally, utterly sorry," I said in my most pathetic voice. "I should never have written those things. I didn't mean to make you sound like a sociopath. And I didn't mean to imply that you want to kick everyone's butt, although—and I say this as your best friend—you do make a lot of threats."

"Have I ever acted on them?" Keisha demanded.

"No, you haven't," I said. "Please, *please* forgive me. I've learned my lesson. I will never, ever write about anyone without their permission again."

Or at least, I'd make sure there was no way anyone else could ever get the password.

Keisha stared at her magazine and flipped another page.

"You can beat me with your magazine," I told her. "And make me watch *Killer Klowns from Outer Space* a hundred times in a row."

Keisha's mouth twitched into something I thought might be a smile. "That's not a punishment."

"It is to me!" I protested.

Keisha started laughing and then I did, too. She whacked me with her magazine.

"That's for being dumb enough to post all that stuff online in the first place," she said.

I sat down on the edge of her bed. "So, what about Roger?"

She blinked at me. "What about him?"

"Keisha, did you read all my blog entries?"

"No, just that one I threw at you."

"So you don't know what any of it said, other than that?" I asked.

"Only what I've heard from other people," she said. "I know you wrote about your crush on Seth."

"But other than that," I said, "you don't know *anything else*?"

Keisha narrowed her eyes. "Why? Did you write something *else* about me?"

I looked at her clock. It was nearing noon. "Come with me to Pizza 'N More," I said.

Keisha tossed her magazine aside and slid off the bed. "Okay. I'm hungry anyway."

I couldn't keep my legs from bouncing as Keisha drove through town. This plan *had* to work.

"What is wrong with you?" Keisha asked. "You're driving me crazy."

"Sorry." I stared out the window as we pulled into the parking lot. Yes! Roger was already there. I saw his car parked near the back.

He was seated in the front corner booth when we walked in. I led Keisha toward him.

"Sit," I instructed Keisha. She did so, giving Roger a confused look.

I turned to Roger. "Keisha doesn't know."

His eyes widened and his face turned white. He was suddenly nervous and reached for his Coke with a shaking hand.

"Know what?" Keisha asked, looking from Roger to me and back again. "What's going on?"

"I'm going to solve this right now," I told them both. "Keisha, Roger Fawcett is your secret admirer. He really likes you and I hope you'll at least give him a chance, because you couldn't find a more perfect guy. He's the greatest cousin I'll ever have. Any girl who snags him should consider herself very lucky. Oh, and he's sorry about the flower beast. He'll never do that again."

Keisha stared at Roger. "You really sent me all that stuff?"

Roger fiddled with the paper from his straw. "Yeah," he said.

A slow smile spread across Keisha's face. "I was hoping it was you."

I glanced up and saw Seth walking across the parking lot toward the building. "I'll leave you two alone. I have other things to do." I sighed, but I was smiling. "My work is never done."

Seth had just stepped into the restaurant when I walked up to him. He smiled when he saw me and my stomach flipped. That smile was for *me*!

He nodded at Keisha and Roger, who were now laughing and talking, and asked, "So he finally told her about the secret admirer stuff?"

I blinked at him. "How did you know about that?"

"Who do you think helped him tape all those hearts to the desk?" He grinned. "I found him that day in the chemistry room. When he explained what he was doing, I offered to help. I kept trying to get him to just *tell* her that he liked her. Of course, he tried to get me to tell you how I felt, too. So I guess we're both better at giving out advice than taking it."

I laughed. "I can't believe you didn't tell me you knew."

"Some of us are better at keeping secrets than others," he said, winking at me.

I swatted at his arm. "How many times do I have to apologize?"

"None, as long as I get to do this." He pulled me toward him and kissed me.

"How do you think you did?" Seth asked as we walked out of chemistry after our midterm on Monday.

"Okay, I hope," I said. "You?"

"I think I did pretty well, thanks to your tutoring."

Uh-oh. There was one last thing I needed to come clean about.

"Seth," I began. "I kind of have to tell you something."

Seth stopped walking and looked down at me, furrowing his brow. "What?"

"Well, I'm not *exactly* very good in chemistry. In fact, when I started tutoring you, I was in danger of failing."

Seth blinked but didn't say anything.

"When you asked me for help, I didn't want to say no, you know, because I really liked you. So I got Keisha to tutor me in the morning and then I tutored you in the afternoon."

Seth blinked again. "You tutored me in a subject that you were almost *failing?*"

I nodded, cringing. "Yeah."

"And my grades have actually been going up, thanks to your tutoring?"

"Um, I guess so."

Seth laughed as he began walking again. "You really are something, you know that?"

SOMETHING TO BLOG ABOUT

I haven't written in this blog in almost three weeks—not since my blog disaster. I've actually missed writing here. The notebook just wasn't the same. And my hand hurt if I wrote too much at once.

I'm at the Riveras' right now, using the computer in Mr. Rivera's home office. I had to get away from everyone because Mr. Rivera keeps trying to make out with my mother in front of me. He leaned over to kiss her earlier and I swear I saw tongue. I had to "accidentally" poke him in the butt with a fork as I was walking by. HELLO! I'M IN THE SAME ROOM! Have some decency for other people's sanity, please.

Oh, I got my midterm results back last week. I passed everything, even chemistry. Seth passed, too, with a B minus, so maybe I'm not so bad at this tutoring thing.

SOMETHING TO BLOG ABOUT

- ABOUT
- RECENT POSTS
- SEPTEMBER
- OCTOBER
- NOVEMBER

SO GOOD-BYE
ISN'T FOREVER

Right now, Mom is in the kitchen making a salad. Mr. Rivera is outside. He's grilling steaks, even though it's way too cold today to be out there cooking. But he insists that Mom and I try his famous Southwestern Steaks, which I discovered is steak soaked in salsa.

Sounds . . . interesting.

Mr. Rivera and Mom both seem to be in a really good mood today and they say they have something important to tell us. I have a feeling I can guess what it is, and you know what? I'm really happy for them. Even if it does mean I'm stuck with Angel and will actually have to—yikes—*live* in the same house as her. I hope we can both make it out alive. And I hope Mr. Rivera cools it with the tongue action.

ANGEL FOUND ME IN THE LIVING ROOM, looking at her second-place ribbon on the mantel.

"Jealous much?" she asked, smirking as she threw herself down on the couch.

I snorted. "Yeah, I'm so jealous I can't make a bright orange whatever the heck that thing is."

"You wouldn't know art if I smacked you on the head with it," Angel told me.

"And you wouldn't know good manners if I shoved them down your throat. I'm a guest in your home. You're supposed to make room for me to sit." I gestured toward the couch, where Angel had stretched her legs out across the cushions.

"Since our parents are planning to tell us they're engaged

tonight, you're not a guest any longer. Fight for a seat or sit on the floor."

I stepped forward, grabbed Angel's ankles, and shoved her legs off the couch. I sat down before she could put her feet back in the way. Angel's days of intimidating me with her nastiness were long over.

"So how are things in paradise?" Angel asked. "Have you and Seth made out?"

I felt my neck grow hot. "I'm not telling you anything about my love life!"

Angel rolled her eyes. "Fine. So I guess you can't be mad at me about the blog anymore, since it finally got the two of you to admit you're crazy for each other. Don't ask me why."

"Oh, no, I'm still mad about that. And believe me, I plan to get my revenge. The blog thing will be pretty hard to top, so I'll need a while to think about it."

I saw a slight smile flicker across Angel's face.

"Girls!" Mom called from the kitchen. "I could use some help in here!"

I started to stand, but Angel jumped up and knocked me back down to the couch.

"Oops. Sorry, Libby!" she said, giggling.

It was the first time she had ever called me Libby. I couldn't think of an adequate response because I was in shock.

"By the way," Angel said as she started toward the kitchen, "that color you're wearing makes you look sickly. Never wear that sweater again."

It was kind of comforting to know that some things would never change, no matter how much everything else did.

THIS BOOK WAS ART DIRECTED by Chad W. Beckerman. The text is set in 12-point Adobe Garamond, a typeface that is based on those created in the sixteenth century by Claude Garamond. Garamond modeled his typefaces on those created by Venetian printers at the end of the fifteenth century. The modern version used in this book was designed by Robert Slimbach, who studied Garamond's historic typefaces at the Plantin-Moretus Museum in Antwerp, Belgium. The display type is Annabelle.